I0628750

VIVACIOUS VIXENS &
BLACKMAIL BABES

Blackmail babes, dangerous dames, femme fatales, manic minxes, saucy strumpets, torrid trollops, vivacious vixens, and white trash wantons—men fall for them, men love them, men hate them, men wish they had never met these bombastic broads!

Here are a novella and four short stories about such dudes, fellows, gentlemen, heels, husbands, killers, and patsies that wind up in trouble when they put their business where their business doesn't belong. See them as they try to squirm out of the messes they have made for themselves, and the strange events that follow—from murder to mayhem, desire to destiny, hell and havoc! One thing's for sure, though: life will never be the same for these poor saps! Great noir reading!

Borgo Press Books by MICHAEL HEMMINGSON

VIVACIOUS VIXENS
&
BLACKMAIL BABES
TALES OF EROTIC NOIR

MICHAEL HEMMINGSON

THE BORGO PRESS
MMXII

VIVACIOUS VIXENS & BLACKMAIL BABES

Copyright © 2011, 2012 by Michael Hemmingson
"Vivacious Vixens" was originally published in *Whodunit? The First Borgo Press Book of Crime and Mystery Stories*, edited by Robert Reginald, Borgo Press, 2011. Copyright © 2011 by Michael Hemmingson

FIRST EDITION

Published by Wildside Press LLC

www.wildsidebooks.com

VIVACIOUS VIXENS &
BLACKMAIL BABES

CONTENTS

VIVACIOUS VIXENS!

1.

It was a good nap. I was dreaming that I had a better life full of money, rye, and women. The busty brunette who woke me up for loving was not my girlfriend, nor was she my wife. She was another man's wife. That man, the fool, was away in New York City on a business trip, allowing us this time together. His name was Paul Fremont.

Her name was Eve. She was twenty-four-years old and had a forty-inch bust, curly black hair, a flat, nineteen-inch stomach, and thirty-six-inch hips, giving her a nice, shapely body any man would be a fool to not take a second glance at. She stood five-seven without heels, and weighed a hundred and ten pounds. She was married to a man twice her age. It was clearly a loveless marriage for money only. Or so she told me.

I reached satisfaction with an enormous shudder, every fiber of my six-foot-two, one-hundred-ninety-pound frame lit up like a town square Christmas tree.

Eve smiled at me, enjoying the pleasure she had provided.

"That was great," I said.

"We aim to please."

"Thank you, ma'am."

"Anytime, anywhere, kind sir."

I looked at my watch.

"Cripes," I said, "it's late. How the hell did that happen?"

'You were napping."

"Why didn't you wake me?"

"You looked so peaceful, snoring away," she said. "You had this baby boy grin and I just couldn't wake you, but then I did, in my special way."

She licked her lips.

"Was having some nice dreams," I said.

I got up to my feet and put my jeans on.

"Was I in your dream world?" she asked.

"Of course," I said. "Who else?"

She jumped up, hugged me, kissed me. I could taste myself on her lips and tongue. "Oh, Jack, I love you like something crazy!"

I said the same.

"Stay, why don't you. Just stay and I'll love you with my mouth all day and night."

We had yet to have actual sex, intercourse. Everything we did in bed, or in her car, was with hands and mouths.

"Gotta get back to work," I told her, kissing her again. "I'm an hour late as is."

"The hell with that crappy job."

"It may be crappy, but it's the only job I have. Some of us have to work for a living, you know."

"I'll take care of you."

"That's what you say now."

"I just want us to be together, always," she said, pouting.

"That day will come," I told her.

"When?"

"Soon."

"Not soon enough."

There were some practical issues to deal with before we could be together as man and wife—her husband, my wife. I was debating about keeping the girlfriend, knowing that eventually there would be a mistress. All married men cheat at one point, as do all married women. It's the way the world works—at least that's how it worked in this neck of the globe, Hittsville, population 30,000, a shabby town on the tri-state border of

Pennsylvania, New York, and New Jersey.

"When will I see you again?" she asked.

"Same time tomorrow?"

"I'll be here, darling."

One last kiss, I patted her on the rear—what a wonderful, hard butt it was—and left the hotel room.

The hotel was two blocks away from the construction site I had been working at three weeks now. I walked there, fast. The foreman, a fellow named Jed, and I didn't get along, and I knew he was going to give me hell for coming back this late.

I had hoped to slip into the job and get back to the cement mixing like I'd been there the whole time, but Jed was waiting for me.

"Card! Jack Card! How *nice* of you to grace us with your pretty face."

I grinned and showed him my pretty teeth that went with the face.

He was a short man in his forties, five foot five and stocky. He had little man's syndrome and enjoyed looking up at taller men and bossing them around, which is what he was doing to me.

"A two-hour lunch?!"

"Sorry about that."

"Think you're something special, Card?"

"Not at all."

"Think you can just take a two-hour lunch and not ask?"

"I'm sorry, Jed, something important came up."

"Important, eh?"

"Yeah."

"How important?"

"A minor emergency."

"Why, then, tell us all about it, boy."

Half the construction crew had stopped what they were doing and they were watching to see what happened.

"It's...personal."

"Personal, my ass."

"Look, it won't happen again."

"Oh I know it won't happen again," he said, "because you're fired!"

"What?"

"I'm canning you, Card."

"Oh, come on."

"Get your gear and move your rear." He thought that was funny and laughed.

I thought he was giving me grief. "Are you serious?"

"Do I look like a comedian?"

"I need this job, Jed."

"So do a lot of guys, guys who respect the job site and take forty-five minutes for lunch like the rest of us."

"Just dock me an hour and fifteen," I said.

"I've had it with you, Card. Ever since day one, I knew you were a clown and would mess up. Should've fired you sooner."

"Look," I said.

"*You* look," he said. "This site is my realm, here I am king and president, and you disrespected it. Who the hell do you think you are?"

I knew he had the right to point this out, just as I knew he had to fire me or else other guys would take long lunches. But I needed this damn job and he knew it.

"What if I came to *your realm* and disrespected *you*, Card?" he went on. "What if I went to your house and started fondling your pretty wife's bosoms, how would you feel? What would you do?"

My blood started to boil. He should have known better—you don't use wives and kids to rile a guy up. It's dangerous.

"Eh?" he said, getting closer to me, pointing his finger. "How would you like it if I went to see your little chippie on the side and had a taste?"

"What?" I clenched my fists.

"Oh, we all know about your side poon, we all know about that teenage tramp you got holed up at Wilma's rooming house."

Small town, a lot of mouths.

"So what if I went over there and got a piece of that whore tail?" he said. "What would you feel, what would you do?"

"I'd do this," and I punched him right in the nose. He stumbled back, blood pouring out of his nostrils. He muttered something and came after me, but I laid two more blows into his face, knocking some teeth out. He fell to the ground, half conscious.

A couple of the guys laughed and cheered me.

I grabbed my tools and walked away.

2.

Jobless is never a good feeling. I thought of going back to the hotel to see if Eve was still there. I didn't see her Cadillac parked. I could always call her at a phone booth. Decided to have a few beers instead. Walked into the bar down the block.

I sat at the counter.

"What'll you have?" asked the bartender, a skinny old guy in his sixties.

"Beer."

"One beer coming up." He put a cold mug in front of me. "Twenty cents."

I dug a quarter out of my pocket and laid it down.

I had two more quarters in my pocket and seven dollars in my wallet. I had maybe fifty in the bank and that was it. Now I didn't have a job.

Here I was: twenty-seven, never finished high school, didn't have any skills beyond general labor. It was the spring of 1957 and I had $52.50 to my name, with a frigid wife to support, a teenage lover to keep, and I was falling for a married woman who spent more money in a day than I did in a month.

Nursing the mug of beer, I thought about how I arrived here to this point of my shabby life: sitting in an empty bar at 2:30 P.M. with a swollen fist, unemployed and going nowhere.

I guess it started with Kay, my wife, when I got her in the family way during high school. She was sixteen and I was seventeen. She did not want to hear abortion. Her folks were none too pleased; her mother wanted to send her away so the family name would not be soiled, and her father wanted to put his old World War II revolver to my temple and pull. Kay and I ran off up north where we eloped, and when we came back there wasn't much to do. In time, her folks warmed up to me—I went hunting and fishing with her dad and her mom, after a few glasses of wine, offered herself up to me, saying, "Give me some of what that tramp girl of mine gets!"

Kay was no tramp, not then anyway. Our baby girl was born a month premature and with a heart condition. She died in her sixth month. The loss nearly destroyed us both, and her folks— her father got drunk one evening and smashed his Plymouth into a tree, his body flying through the windshield. He died instantly. Her mother was sent to a sanatorium and is still there, paid for by money from a life insurance policy that Kay's father had taken out on himself. If her mother wasn't in there, some of that money would have gone to Kay.

Kay and I drank like fish and fought like Huns. We blamed each other, we blamed ourselves. Then she wanted another baby. She was only seventeen but she wanted a replacement. We tried, we tried a lot, we tried until we were blue. For years it didn't happen.

"God is punishing us," she said, "he took our one baby and now he won't let us have another."

Or: "There's something wrong with your soldiers, Jack. They're 4-F! They're not doing their duty and hitting the mark!"

That's when she started to hit the bars when I was gone. I was driving a delivery truck then, so I was away a lot. She'd pick up men and take them back to their motel rooms or to our place. All she wanted them for was their seed, so she could have another baby.

It still didn't happen.

Sometimes I'd come home and find a strange man sleeping in my bed. I'd wake him and kick him out. I wasn't out looking for a fight. I wasn't mad at Kay either. I wasn't being faithful and she no longer wanted me.

Have no idea why we remained married, ten years now. I guess we were a habit, we didn't know how to be without each other, without the anger and the yelling and the memories.

I'm not sure when I began writing stories. I got into buying pulp magazines from the newsstands and the pharmacies. Science-fiction, westerns, detective tales. I loved them and wanted to write some of my own.

One day I bought an old typewriter for three dollars, some paper, carbons, and started writing short stories. The first were only two or three pages long, then they started to come in at ten or fifteen pages, some twenty.

Kay thought it was a silly waste of time until I sold one, a Western, for a penny a word. It was 3,000 words, so that was $30. Then she started to think I could be a writer, and she wanted a baby again and we tried...and nothing.

Writing was a side thing. I'd mail the stories out or sometimes I would go into New York City for the hell of it, just to get away, and walk my stories in. Some of the pulps let you do that. You'd make an appointment, the editor would take fifteen minutes or so reading what you had, and he'd either nod his head yes or no after. Yes, his secretary would cut you a check for $30-$50, depending on the length of the tale and what the magazine paid. If no, you went somewhere else, or mailed it out to lesser pulps in New Jersey or Chicago.

That's when Lucy came into the picture. I had just delivered some goods and decided to drive the truck into the city and take some stories around. I didn't want to be at home with Kay's drinking and yelling. I spotted this young girl on the side of the road, her thumb out, a suitcase in her other hand.

"Stop," I said to myself.

I stopped for her. She was blonde and compact. She said she was seventeen and I believed her. It wasn't until much later that I found out she was fourteen, when it was too late.

She was headed for the city. She wanted to try her hand at modeling and acting. She had the dream so many had. I thought she could make it: she was pretty and sexy enough, better than some models I'd seen.

I got a cheap room at the Chelsea Hotel, where I always stayed when in New York. I'd hit the pulps in the morning. I had seven short stories to sell.

Lucy shared the room with me, as she had no money. We got some dinner and she read two of my stories and said they were good. "You'll be famous one day," she said.

"You too," I said.

"The model and the writer," she said, "how romantic is that?"

She did not object to sharing my bed, and I didn't have any trouble with the arrangement either, although she was seventeen and I had some reservations.

"I'm old enough for you, dear," she whispered, grabbing my hand and putting it on her right breast.

She was. She was a hellcat hellion in the sack. She did things no other girl I ever knew did. She did things no decent man and woman would ever do to each other. She knew strange and dirty ways to use her mouth and hands.

That night, she cried and told me she was running away from home, from a disgusting stepfather who had been having her since she was eleven and sometimes "rented" her out to carnivals or parties, where she was made to drink and then dance in front of a group of men who would touch her with their grubby hands.

I felt anger. I wanted to kill this man who did that to her.

"I believe in destiny, Jack," she said. "We were meant to meet and I was meant to be yours. I love you, Jack!"

That day, I made my rounds and sold three stories. I was feeling high—the sales, the beautiful girl in my room, the city of many possibilities!

I almost didn't expect her to be there when I returned, but she was, and she was naked on the bed.

"I'm all yours," she said, opening her legs.

I jumped.

I jumped in deep.

Too deep, maybe. She didn't want to stay in New York after all. She wanted to go back to Hittsville with me and become my wife.

I told her I was married. She looked like she wanted to punch me. I then told her it was a bad marriage and Kay was a bad wife, that I really wasn't married in heart and soul, just on paper.

"So you'll divorce her," Lucy said. "I can wait."

She's been waiting for two years now.

For two years, she has been living in a rooming house on the south side of town, a good three miles from where I lived with Kay. Since she looked old enough, she told Wilma, who ran the house, she was seventeen, and Wilma thought she was now nineteen. So did the owner of the diner where she worked part-time. I mostly paid for everything—the room ($10 a week), food and clothes (another $10), but she needed her own money. She said she was saving it for when we got married.

Why was Lucy willing to wait this long? The girl had no sense of time—two days and two weeks were the same to her. These past two years were like two months in her mind.

She'd say, "I'm patient, I know there are things you need to take care of before the divorce."

Somehow, I just fell into this pattern with Lucy: I would go see her or I'd go home. Kay never asked where I was, and she didn't come home some nights either.

Two months ago, I met Eve and my life changed again.

I was doing a short paint job. There's a contractor I know who calls me up whenever he needs an extra man or two, which isn't often, but the extra money always comes in handy. The house was in a town five miles east in Evanstown, mostly a lot of big houses dating back to the 1800s. I was on a ladder, happily painting away, thinking about Lucy and our future, when I saw her from the window: she walked into the room, a towel wrapped around her sultry, smooth body. Her back was turned to me. She dropped the towel and opened a dresser drawer, took out a bra and pair of panties—they were both light blue—and slowly put them on.

I nearly fell off the ladder I was so astounded. I knew I should have stepped down the ladder, not looking, but I was too mesmerized, I was frozen by the sight of her. I had never seen a woman with a more perfect body. Kay was average and pretty, but alcohol was making parts of her sag. Lucy was still a kid and growing, and one day, in her twenties, she might look like Eve, but I had my doubts.

She turned and saw me.

We stared at each other.

She cracked a little smile and left the room.

She seemed to wiggle her rear end for my benefit.

Or was that just my imagination?

Her name was Eve Fremont. She was twenty-six-years old, blonde, and married to sixty-year-old Paul Fremont of Fremont Enterprises. Her husband was loaded—he owned several restaurants, a frozen food distribution company, a life and car insurance company, and a small radio station between Hittsville and Evanstown.

I didn't see her the rest of that day. I was afraid she would accuse me of being a peeping tom. I saw her husband, and kept expecting him to slug me or call the police; instead, he approved of the progress of the job. He said he had to go into New York on business for a few days, and was looking forward to seeing the job completed.

Away for a few days. That meant his wife, Eve, would be alone here.

Or maybe she was going with him?

"Need anything, just ask my wife, okay?" Fremont said.

So she would be here.

And as luck would have it, I was working alone on the job the next day, mostly doing touch-ups and sanding down bumps.

She came out of the house wearing a long blue robe and carrying a folded towel.

I started to sweat.

"How is everything going, Mr...? Did I get your name?" she asked.

My mouth was dry.

"Card," I said. "Jack Card."

"How are things going with the paint job, Jack?"

"Just fine, Mrs. Fremont."

"I'll let my husband know when he calls, that all is fine," she said. "And all is fine," she added, looking me up and down and smiling.

My knees felt weak.

"Do you need anything? Water? Soda? Beer?"

"No thank you, Mrs. Fremont," I said.

"Well, if you need anything, let me know," she said. "I'll be right over here, working on my tan."

Tan?

She spread a towel on the front lawn and removed her robe. She was wearing a black bikini. I dropped my paint brush when I got a look at that body. I had seen her body naked, and now this—both were magnificent to my eyes.

But it was hard to work. I couldn't focus on painting because I kept turning to look at her lying in the sun. She changed positions every ten minutes: first she was on her back, and then on her stomach, and then on her back.

After about an agonizing hour of this display of flesh, I heard her voice: "Mr. Card? Jack? Jack, are you around?"

"Yes, ma'am, I'm here."

"Ma'am. Oh dear lord, none of that. Could you come here, please?"

"Um, yes, sure, one minute."

I placed the paint roller down, looked at my hands and arms, covered in paint, as well as my jeans and shirt. Why did I have to look like some working-class nobody? Because I was.

I thought my legs were going to give out under me when I approached her. She was hoisted up on her elbows. Her stomach was flat and tan, her legs smooth, muscular, and tan, her neck sweaty and tan.

"There you are," she said. "Are you thirsty?"

"Well, Mrs. Fremont, I...." I what?

"Call me Eve, will you?"

"Sure...Eve."

"I'm thirsty. Would you be a dear, Jack, and go inside to the fridge and get me a can of beer? Grab yourself one too if you wish."

"Sure...Eve."

I went into the house. I had to idea where the kitchen was inside this mansion, but it wasn't too hard to find. The kitchen was tiled and sparkled clean. I had never seen such an immaculate kitchen. Kay never kept the kitchen tidy, or the apartment; it was always filled with stacked dishes going back two weeks, empty cans and bottles, leftover food attracting flies and ants.

The lower portion of the fridge was packed with beer cans. I grabbed two. I went back outside.

Handed her a can.

"Good, you got one for yourself," she said. "Who wants to drink alone?"

She pressed the cold can to her cheek. "Nice." She moved the can to her neck, then down to her chest. She looked at me. "Nice," she said. "So hot out."

"Umm," was all I could manage.

She opened the car. Some of it sprayed onto her chest and face. She giggled.

I opened my can.

"Would you do me a favor, Jack?"

"Certainly."

"I got beer on myself...."

"I can get you a towel," I said.

"I need you to do something else."

"Yes?"

"Come down here and lick the beer off me."

"What?"

She laughed. "Can't believe your ears, Jack? That wasn't your imagination and this isn't a dream. I want you to lick this beer off my skin. And then I want you to kiss me. And then I want you to make me."

I didn't hesitate. I took the plunge. I tossed my beer can aside and fell down to the ground with her, grabbed her, and began licking. I licked her chest and my right hand caressed one of her glorious, hard breasts. She did not object.

I licked the beer off her neck.

We started to kiss.

"Inside?" I said.

"Right here," she said.

"Outside, here?"

"No one's around, no one will see," she said. "This is my home. I've done it plenty of times."

Not with her husband, I was certain of that. How many men had this wanton wench seduced? I didn't care. I was living for the moment. I took her right there on the grass. Eve was born to be made, and I made her twice on the grass, twice with splendor, twice with the promise of more.

That's how it started. After the paint job, I started meeting her in various places. Sometimes we'd have fun in her car, or go to a motel outside Hittsville. When I took the construction job two weeks ago, she would get a room, and I would meet her during lunch break for a quickie and after work for a couple of hours, and then I would either go see Lucy or go home to Kay, and Eve would go home to her rich husband.

I hated her husband and all he had—not just all that money, but the young wife he obviously could not satisfy. Eve told me several times how she avoided intimacy at night, and sometimes she slept in one of the guest rooms.

"He's too old to get the blood flowing anyway," she said, "but sometimes he gets randy, and it makes me sick. His body, all that white hair, and he's not very big, if you know what I mean."

I knew what she meant.

"A woman likes to feel filled in order to reach fulfillment," she said, and added in a vixen voice, "You're big, Jack, and I most certainly like that."

"Is it really that important?"

"For some girls, yes. For some girls, it makes all the difference."

"Especially if they sleep around a lot."

"I'm not like that."

"Not now."

"I had my times when I was younger."

"How young?"

"Wouldn't you like to know."

"How old were you, the first time?" I asked.

She replied, "Wouldn't you like to know."

"Why did you marry him?" I asked. "and don't you dare say 'wouldn't you like to know'."

"Why do you think?"

"Just for the money?"

"I hated being a waitress. I wanted more in life. I was tired of dating poor men."

"Like me?"

"Not like you. Men who—had no ambition, men who would never be anybody. You have ambition."

"I do?"

"You write those short stories. One day you'll write a novel."

"I doubt it."

"Why not?"

"I don't have the time to write a novel. Stories are easy—I can write one in a day, two days. Novels take time." This wasn't true. I knew a man who lived in a trailer on the edge of town. He wrote novels and they were on all the racks and newsstands. He'd written at least a hundred novels in the past ten years. He told me most took two weeks, a chapter a day, fourteen-chapter books. "When I was ten years younger," he'd said, "I could do two or three chapters a day and have a book done in six days." His name was Roger Weaver.

Back to Eve.

She said, "I won't lie. Paul was nice to me. He romanced me. He offered a better life."

"He offered money," I said.

"Less struggle, less lack of security," she said.

I understood.

"You don't hold it against me," she said.

"We do what we have to do."

"You're married."

"Some marriage."

"We both offer one another something we both need, something we don't get at home."

She didn't know about Lucy.

"It's a good arrangement, don't you think?"

Yes, it was.

"You're always happy after," she said.

Yes, I was.

"And I'm fulfilled," she said.

Yes, she was.

* * * * * * *

I left the bar at 3:30 and drove my beat-up Plymouth to Wilma's boarding house. Gas was low and the muffler was making kicking sounds. The brake pads were almost gone. I had no idea how much longer this car would last, and I was surprised it had lasted this long. It would never survive another trip to New York. I'd take the train. Lucy liked the train.

Wilma was sweeping the porch of the house. She was a short woman, barely five feet tall, with dark hair and chiseled looks. She was in her fifties. I knew she was a knock-out little hellion when she was a teenager, and in her twenties. There were photos from her modeling days hung in the hallways. She went to Hollywood for awhile, but that didn't work out; and when her mother died and left the house in the will, Wilma stayed, and opened up the seven rooms for rent.

She looked up from her sweeping. "Well, well, well, you," she said.

"Wilma."

"You're here early."

"Short day."

"You get canned?"

"Short day."

"I know the look of a man whose been fired, and you got that look."

"The rent's always on time."

"Yes it is, and Lucy is a good tenant, quiet, never brings strange men home, other than your handsome self."

"Thanks."

"She's not here."

"Lucy?"

"Who else?"

"Where is she?"

Wilma shrugged. "She went out around noon."

This wasn't one of her days at the diner. This was unlike her—there's nothing more Lucy liked but to lay in bed all day and watch the TV.

"Wanna drink while you wait?" Wilma asked me.

"What do you have?"

"Cold wine, cold beer, rye and ice cubes."

I'd had enough beer at the bar, and this drink was free. "Rye would be nice," I said.

She went inside. I sat in one of the four chairs on the porch. It was still hot out, but the sun would set in an hour or so.

Wilma returned with a glass with three shots of rye and three ice cubes. She had a glass of red wine.

We toasted.

"To all your yesterdays and all our dreams," she said.

Why not.

I drank and brooded.

"You thinking she has another man?" said Wilma.

I was thinking about my lack of a job. "She's not the type," I said. The truth: after two years, I had no idea what type Lucy was. She was sixteen going on seventeen; she still had to grow into a woman, even if she looked like one. She passed for nine-teen/twenty and that's what Wilma figured she was. If Wilma knew the truth, she would have never rented the room out; if she knew now, she would probably kick Lucy out and call the cops on me for statutory rape.

"She loves you crazy like," said Wilma. "And she's a good girl."

"She is."

"She has quite the body on her."

"She does."

"She shouldn't be a waitress. She should be a model, an actress with that body, you know?"

"Like you were?"

"I could warn her of the pitfalls, I been down the road," Wilma said. "I've tried warning girls before, but they all think they're immune to the evils of modeling. They just have to find out on their own."

"Or get married."

"Or that."

Or give up, I thought, or become strippers and hookers.

Wilma finished her glass of wine and said, "So when are you going to marry her and the two of you get a real home, an apartment, or a house, fill it with rugrats?"

"We're getting there. There's plenty of time." If Wilma knew I had a wife, and a lover on the side, I wouldn't be so welcome to her booze and porch.

"She's still young—and speaking of the she-devil...," Wilma nodded for me to look.

Lucy was down the block, walking toward the rooming house. She wore a pale green summer dress, sandals, and a hat. The dress clung tightly to her body, causing attention to the way she swayed her hips and rear end as she walked.

"I'll leave you two love-birds alone," Wilma said. She stood, grabbed her broom, and left the porch.

"Jack," Lucy said with a confused smile, "you're here."

"Yep."

"Early."

"Yep."

She appeared uncomfortable. "What's going on, Jack?"

"Where were you?"

"Went into town."

"Walked?"

"The bus."

"That far?"

"Yeah," she said.

I knew Wilma was listening to us. "Let's go inside," I said.

"Okay," she said.

In the room, I hugged her. She didn't respond as she usually did. She sighed.

Something was wrong.

"Did you lose your job, Jack?"

"Yeah."

"I figured."

"I'll find work."

"Work is scarce."

"Don't worry."

"I have to worry now," she said, moving away from me.

I sat on the bed and watched her. She took the summer dress off. She stood before me in her bra and panties.

She looked at herself in the mirror on the wall, observing herself forward and on each side.

"You're beautiful, as always, baby," I said.

"Thank you, Jack. I hope you'll always say that."

"Okay, something ain't right," I said. "Why were you in town?"

"Do you think I was seeing a man?" she asked.

"I don't know what to think."

"You don't trust me?"

"I trust you."

"Do you love me?"

"You know the answer."

"Say it."

"I love you, Lucy."

"Say it again."

I said it again.

"Again."

I did.

"How much do you love me?" She was still standing in front of the mirror, looking at me in the reflection.

"As much as the whole galaxy."

"That's all?"

"Universe," I said. "You can't get any bigger than that. Toss in some parallel universes, too."

"That's good, because I have to know, what I'm about to tell you."

I was feeling nervous. "Just tell me, Lucy."

"I went to see the doctor in town," she said.

A chill went up my spine. She didn't need to spill it—now it made sense, her moodiness, her looking at her body in the mirror, seeing if it showed yet.

"I'm pregnant," she said.

I nodded.

"Well, Jack?"

"How far are you?"

"Almost seven weeks."

"How did this happen?"

"You know how, being careless as we get sometimes."

"Oh boy," I said. A pregnant girlfriend, a wife depressed because she couldn't get pregnant, and me with $52.50 to my name.

"Jack? What are you thinking?"

I gave my best smile. "In some ways, this is a beautiful thing."

"And in other ways?"

"Well, what do you want to do?"

"I won't have an abortion," she said.

"Okay."

"So? Jack?"

"Looks like we're having a family, baby doll."

She sighed, relieved. She came to me. She sat in my lap. I kissed her. She placed my hand on her belly.

"Do you want a boy or girl?" she asked softly.

"Doesn't matter. As long as the baby is healthy and lives." I felt some pain, thinking of my little daughter and her bad heart.

"I'd like a boy," she said.

"A boy is good," I said.

"A girl has to deal with a lot of bad things in the world," she said. "A girl will have a body that people will have designs on."

"Hush," I said, and kissed her.

"Jack?"

"Um."

"Now you have to divorce Kay, because we have to get married now. I won't have a bastard baby."

"I know," I said.

We kissed. I removed her bra.

"Wait," she said.

"You can't get in trouble twice, the same time," I said, amused.

"Not that." She got up and checked the blinds, made sure they were tightly shut. "Just in case."

"Wilma has no desire to watch us," I said.

"Jack...this morning...I was *sure* someone was out there, looking in."

"Was a cat. A rodent."

"No, I could feel some eyes on me. And when I went to check, I swore I heard feet running away."

"Your hormones," I said. "Your imagination."

"No, Jack, it's just like that night a week ago. I think there's a peeping tom running about."

"No," I said, "peeping toms are a myth."

"My stepfather liked to prowl and look into windows," she said. "Then he'd come home late with his blood boiling and he'd come to my bed...."

"Hush," I said. Thinking about her stepfather raping her did no good for love-making.

"Hold me, Jack!" she said, clinging to my arms.

I held her.

"Never let go," she said.

"Hush, baby."

"Baby," she said, "we're going to have a *baby.*"

Then we did what people do to make babies and it was nice, very nice, like it always was with my teenage lover.

3.

I stayed the night. In the morning, Lucy put her uniform on and went to work. I drove across town to my apartment, wondering if my wife would be sober or drunk, alive or dead.

Kay seemed sober and I was surprised. She was dusting the place. The apartment looked better than it usually did.

She stopped what she was doing when she noticed me watching her. "You're home," she said.

"Yes, I am. What's...going on?"

"Cleaning up."

"That's new."

"Don't start with me."

"You seem sober."

"I am sober."

"That's new."

"Don't," she said, and sighed. "I have no idea what you think of me, what you tell people, but it's not true."

"The place looks good," I said.

She smiled. "Thanks. Feels good to tidy up. Jack?"

"Yeah."

"Why didn't you come home last night?"

"You never noticed or cared before," I said. "Did *you* even come home last night?"

"I was here, I was here alone and I was wishing you were here because I was really scared, Jack."

"Scared? Why?"

"Let me show you something."

She took me to the back door in the kitchen, outside and down the stairs. We lived on the second floor of the apartment building. She pointed to the bathroom window, and the ladder placed against the wall, by the window.

"Someone was watching me take a bath last night," Kay said.

"Nonsense," I said.

"Why is that ladder there?"

"Could be any reason. Did you talk to the landlady?"

"No. I don't want to speak to that bitch. I want to know who's been peeping into the window and looking at me. This isn't the first time, Jack. There have been a couple of other times the past week or so that I thought I was being watched. At first I thought it was you playing games. Then last night I saw a shadow of a head move at the window, and I could see two eyes. I yelled at the head and eyes, Jack, I yelled, 'Hey, what the hell are you doing?' The head and eyes disappeared. I was afraid to go outside and look, but I did and saw the ladder there. I checked this morning, and the ladder is still there. I'm afraid to go to the bathroom or brush my teeth, Jack. I needed you to be here, to protect me, to catch whoever it is doing this."

"Well, you're fine now, you're safe."

We went back inside. I checked the fridge for food or beer. There was a green apple. I took that.

"Jack, why aren't you at work?" my wife asked.

"I'm heading there now," I lied.

"Why did you even bother coming home?"

"Man needs clean clothes," I said, wondering if there were any. I went into the bedroom. I looked at the bed and it was made, neat. Wondered if she had a man in my bed last night, any day this week. Her peeper was most likely some one-night stand she had, or someone she rejected, although I found it hard to believe she turned down any fellow willing to pay for drinks.

I had some clean shirts and one pair of jeans, some socks too. It was nice to get into some clean clothes. I thought about a shower but decided to shower in the hotel room later on.

Kay was sitting on the sofa, waiting for me.

"Stay home today," she said.

"I need to work," I told her.

"Do you have any money?"

"What?"

"I'm flat broke, Jack."

"I gave you fifty bucks last week."

"It's gone."

"Where to?"

"Bills."

"Bills, right," I said. "More like booze. Is that why you're sober? You can't buy any beer or vodka?"

"Oh, Jack, please don't ridicule me," she said, a tear in her eye.

"You have no problem getting men to buy the booze," I said.

"Jack, I'm hungry. I was going to eat that apple as a treat, when I finished the housework."

I wanted to run out of there. Why did I even come here, pay the rent? To keep some clean clothes and boots? I pulled out my wallet. Two dollars. I gave her the bills.

"That's it?"

"All I have right now."

"Will you bring back some more?"

"Two bucks will get you breakfast and a couple of beers."

"We need to talk, Jack," she said.

"I have to go."

"Talk later."

"Later then," and I left her there with my gas money.

Driving nowhere, I thought about the best way for a divorce, and I thought about all the bills a baby would bring. My dead daughter was expensive, with all the doctor visits and the labor, and then the funeral. She was buried in the infants' section of the Hittsville Cemetery.

Turned on the radio and wondered where I could go to find work. It was too late for the day labor hall, you had to check in at five in the morning and wait, with a dozen or so other men, to be called for a job that could last two hours or two days, and if you were lucky, two weeks; if God was smiling on you, two months, but that had never happened to me. I'd have to get up damn early tomorrow, and that meant staying at the apartment. At Lucy's, we always stayed up past midnight, having fun with out bodies and watching late-night television on whatever channel came in on her little black and white set I bought her for her last birthday. "I could see myself on TV one day," Lucy always said.

The local news came on, stuff about the weather and a bank robbery in Syracuse, and maybe the robbers were hiding out in these parts.

And then something about reports of a prowler.

"Several women have called the police about a prowler at their windows, mostly during the night at the hours between midnight and three A.M. Police are on the alert and remind everyone to check your blinds and lock your window before going to bed."

And like that—snap!—it all clicked together, it all made sense. Lucy wasn't imagining things, and Kay's ladder was there for a reason. They weren't the only women targeted. I knew who the prowler was, and why.

"Roger," I said to myself.

I turned the car around.

I needed to pay the old novelist a visit.

* * * * * * *

Roger Weaver lived in an old aluminum trailer in a park on the west side of town. It was a dilapidated place that had few tenants. It was a miracle if the water or electricity worked. I think he paid $10 a month to park there.

Why he lived in such destitute conditions was beyond me, since I knew he was getting between $500-$800 for every novel, with a $200 bonus when there was a second printing or a foreign translation. That's what he told me. But writing two novels a month, Roger was pulling in at least a grand, maybe sixteen hundred or two thousand, including the sale of short stories and nature articles.

Roger worked twelve hours a day, from seven A.M. to seven P.M., taking a half hour for lunch and a half hour to answer mail from his agent or publishers. He did not have a phone, did not wish for one, and couldn't have had one out here anyway. There were no phone lines. He usually paid whatever kids were around the park to run the packages with his manuscripts to the post office, or if I came around, I'd take his mail for him.

I met him though a mutual editor of a crime digest I sold a couple of stories to. The editor asked if I knew Roger Weaver, who lived in the same parts I did. I said I didn't know him, but I had read him and was a fan. I'd heard he was some kind of recluse.

The editor put us together. I was nervous to meet him. He was a legend as far as I was concerned. He'd been at it for fifteen or twenty years, with most of his output from the last ten. Two or three novels by him came out each month, under his name or a variety of pseudonyms, in every genre possible: westerns, crime, detective, softcore sex, true confessions, science-fiction, nurse romances, and teen adventures. He was best known for his dirty books; they sold the most and had great titles like *Tramp Wife in White Shorts and Yellow Halter*, *Hellcat Hellion on Sin Campus*, *Shame Underwear*, *Death Bra*, *My Wife Is a Man*, and *Inbred Hussy*. The men in his books were heels, louses, con men, punks, drunks, detectives, and hired hands; the women were sluts, wenches, bitches, bad wives, frigid wives, and homicidal wives. In other words, just like everyone you meet in any tawdry town or shabby street.

I could hear his Corona typewriter clacking away inside the trailer. He claimed eighty words a minute, hunting and pecking with two fingers. I admired and envied the man for his commitment and energy. I'd never have either, so it was short stories for the rest of my life.

I knocked on the door.

The typing stopped.

His scratchy old voice: "Yeah, who the hell is it?"

"It's me, Roger."

"Who?"

"Jack."

"Eh? Eh, Jack! Come in, boy, come in! It ain't locked!"

I walked in, immediately smelling the odd mixture of coffee, cigarettes, stale beer, and musty old pulp paper. He had copies of his books and other cheap paperbacks stacked three feet high in every possible space in the tiny trailer.

Roger Weaver sat at the card table, behind his typewriter and piles of typing paper: one the current work, one blank sheets, one carbons, one yellow sheets for the carbon copy. He was fifty-one or -two, but sometimes he said he was forty-five or forty-eight, depending on his mood. He was a short man, standing five foot six, balding with a pot belly. He was wearing boxer shorts and a tank top and I was glad he was dressed; he once told me he wrote in the buff when he felt in the mood.

He didn't get up. "Good to see you, Jack, my boy."

"Roger."

"Wanna beer?"

"Why not."

"Help yourself, kid."

I opened the fridge. Stuffed with three different brands of beer. Kay would be in heaven here; she'd probably move in with the old guy if he kept her in supply. He could afford Kay better than I could.

I opened a beer and sat down on the chair across from him. Roger never drank beer during the day, when he worked. He drank cup after tall cup of iced coffee, though, and smoked like cigarettes were going to be banned any minute now. That was his process. Me, I liked to eat carrots and celery when I wrote.

"Say, shouldn't you be at work?" he asked.

"Canned."

"It happens."

"Too often."

"You'll land on your feet, you always do."

"Yeah."

"Maybe a good time to work on that first novel."

"Speaking of which," I said, "how is your current one going?"

"Going real good, real good, I'm pleased so far," he said, looking at the sheet of paper rolled in the typewriter.

"Is it the peeping tom book?"

His good nature changed to ice. "Why do you ask, Jack?"

"I know how you are about research," I said. "When you did the book about the nudists, you joined a nudist camp. When you wrote about the ins and outs of call girls, you paid a few for their time. When you wrote about transvestites, you bought a wardrobe of women's clothes."

"What're you getting at?"

"I'll just come out and say it, Roger." I cleared my throat. "Have you been prowling and peeping lately?"

He made a face. He got up and grabbed a beer from the fridge. This was unlike him, drinking this early.

"Roger," I said.

"It's research, I'm not a pervert."

"Have you been peeking in on Lucy and Kay?"

"I was going to ask you first, but does a peeper ever ask to peep? No, he just does it."

I stood up. "Jesus, Roger, my wife and my girlfriend?"

"I knew where they lived, I knew the set-up. It's harmless, really."

"How?"

"I'm not really a peeping tom, is how."

"But you're doing it!"

"I don't get my jollies from it!" he said, drinking the beer. "Look, it's a sick thing, but in order to write from a peeper's point of view and make it true, I have to get under a peeper's skin."

"Why not interview one?"

"Know any?"

I sat back down. "No more, Roger. Okay? No more Lucy, no more Kay—you're scaring them, and if you get caught...."

"I have no intention of getting caught."

"Who else's windows you been peeping in? I heard on the

radio, the cops are looking for a prowler."

"I branched out."

"I suggest stopping now, before they grab you, and the judge ain't gonna buy this 'it's just research' line, and it could ruin your reputation."

"Or help sales on this book—written by a real peeping tom!"

"Just for one novel?"

"I'll use a new pen name."

"You're crazy, Roger, you know."

"I know."

"I have your word, you'll stop?"

"With Kay and Lucy, yes. But I need to do a little more...there are others...."

"Be careful, then."

"I'm always careful. How about you?"

"Me what?"

"You being careful?" he asked.

"Of course," I lied, thinking of the baby growing inside Lucy.

I would have stayed longer but Roger gets irritated if his writing is interrupted for more than half an hour before 7 P.M. Besides, I needed to rendezvous with Eve at the hotel.

I was there first. The day clerk handed me the key. Eve paid weekly on the room so it could always be available at any time. She also paid the clerks to look the other way and keep their mouths shut, since she was the wife of a prominent businessman in Hittsville. This was the kind of place where discretion is honored, and many married men and women and working girls spent time.

I took my shirt off and looked at myself in the bathroom mirror. My chest and stomach were still tight, but I thought I might have to cut back on the beer or do more sit-ups.

I took a long shower. It felt good.

I lay on the bed and waited.

Eve was there half an hour later. She didn't have that smile and lust in her eyes she usually had. She appeared distraught. She had today's newspaper in her hand.

"I'm so glad you're here," she said.

"Hey, what's wrong?" I sat up. She sat next to me.

She hugged me.

"You smell nice," she said. "Feel nice. So strong. You would protect me."

"Okay, what's going on?"

"Did you read this morning's paper?"

"They must have canceled my subscription," I said. What kind of question was that? I never read the paper. I didn't even read the pulp magazines that published my stories.

She showed me a story on the front page. "Something happened to Paul on his way back from New York."

I read the story, accompanied by a photo of Paul Fremont, the same one he used for his advertisements. Paul Fremont, 62, was driving on the outskirts of town when he saw a car on the side of the road. The car looked like it was having engine trouble, with the hood up, and a young lady was standing beside it. "Being the good Samaritan that I am," Fremont told police, "I stopped to see if I could be of assistance." Upon getting out of his car and approaching the young lady, Fremont was ambushed by two males, unknown age, who hit him several times with their fists and a stick. They took his money and his car, leaving him on the side of the road.

His car was later found three miles away, and on the ground was a couple in their forties who were not as lucky as Fremont— they had been beaten to death when their car was stolen.

The car Fremont had stopped for had been stolen in Syracuse, driven by the three bank robbery suspects.

"I heard about the bank job on the radio," I said.

Eve lit two cigarettes and gave me one. She seldom smoked. She exhaled.

"The world is crazy," she said.

"It always was."

"Is it getting crazier?"

"Probably."

"Hold me."

I held her.

"Kiss me."

I kissed her.

"Love me."

Our bodies came together and it was fantastic like it was always fantastic.

"We're good together," she said, her naked body pressed against my naked body, her hand playing with the hair on my chest.

I had to agree.

"I can't take it anymore, Jack, being with him, his ugly body, the way he smells, the way he passes gas at night, everything about him I hate—and I want out, I want out yesterday."

"Divorce him," I said.

"He'd never give me one, not without a big fight, and he certainly would make sure I got nothing, or very little. You know my tastes, Jack. We wouldn't have this room and time to be together without his damn money."

I had to agree, but I had nothing to say.

"Jack," she said, propping herself up on an elbow and looking straight at me, "I have an idea. It's a crazy idea, but it's a crazy world and I think it could work."

Somehow, I knew what she was going to say before she said it, maybe because I was thinking it myself.

"If Paul could have kept that story out of the paper, he would have. He was even yelling at the paper's editor this morning, something about his money not being good enough. I think he tried paying them off to cut the story; it's what he does. This is a giant embarrassment for him. It's a smear on his manhood. It makes him look—the way he put it, 'I look like a pansy'!"

"I can see how such a thing could hurt a man," I said.

"Why did he stop for that car? 'Good Samaritan,' my left foot!"

"And what a *gorgeous* left foot," and I made a move to go down and kiss said foot.

She grabbed me. "Listen to me, Jack! He stopped because

of the girl. He sees a girl, thinks she's alone, that's what they want a man to think: help the girl, get her made. Instead he gets his ass whopped, his wallet emptied, his car stolen, left on the ground like road kill. He's livid, Jack. He has his guns out. He plans on driving up and down the roads in and out of town tonight to look for them."

"Ridiculous. Those people would be insane to go out and try that again."

"Of course."

"He must know this."

"He's not thinking straight," she said. "And this could be his downfall."

This is when she told me about her idea, her plan. It would take deviant craftiness, but it would free her from her marriage, leaving her a wealthy widow. Then we could be together, and have all his money to spend and live comfortably on.

Her plan meant that we would become criminals.

Murderers.

I thought about it and thought about my miserable shabby life for two minutes, and then said, "Okay, let's do it."

4.

I needed a job tending bar like I needed seven toes on each foot. But when you have $10 in the bank and fifty cents in your pocket, a girl waiting for you in a room, a tramp lush wife in an apartment, you get what you can take. What was so bad about being a bartender? There were the tips, sure, and the base pay, and there was the booze—the booze was the problem. I knew I wouldn't be able to stay away from it, and sure enough, I could not.

Second, the bar was The Dells, located in the Dell, the worst part of this godforsaken shabby town; filled with whores, rough-necks, crooked cops, and lousy drunks.

The kind of people I'd been trying to get away from all my

life.

Third, Eve secured the job for me. Seems Paul held the note on the place and he often spent time there; he never had to pay for drinks and he seemed to like the atmosphere, where, Eve assured me, he slept with a whore now and then.

My job was to spy on him and determine the best time to take care of things, to put her plan into motion.

Eve had told the owner, a fellow in his forties named Scott, that I was a distant cousin of hers and really needed a job, part-time was okay. Scott needed an employee like he needed another rugrat (he told me he had six), but he couldn't say no to Eve—not when she put on the charm, and not when her husband could call in the loan any time he felt like it and take the bar away.

"You really some cousin of Mrs. Fremont's?" Scott asked me the first night of work.

"Does it matter?" I said.

He shrugged. "Guess not; always happy to oblige Mrs. Fremont. She's the obliging type," he said with a wink. "If you know what I mean."

"No," I said, "I don't know what you mean."

"She's a looker."

"I wouldn't know."

"My foot," he said. "You say you don't look?"

"She's my cousin."

"*Is* she?"

"It'd be incest."

"They say it's the best," he said, and laughed.

I laughed too, ha, ha.

"So you *know* Mr. Fremont?" he asked.

I shrugged.

"He used to come in here two, three nights a week. He likes to look at the girls. Hell, who doesn't? What he does is his business. We're all married men with needs, but if I had his wife, I would never need another thing in my life."

I shrugged again.

"Now he's in here every night," Scott said. "What happened

to him last week has him all riled up. The fellow's gonna have a heart attack if he keeps it up. He's pretty steamed."

"You mean when he got robbed?" I asked.

"Mr. Fremont is not used to being on that end of the stick."

I was all broken up inside for him.

Scott said, "He wants revenge something bad, I tell you."

There was something I wanted bad: his wife, his life, his money. I wouldn't be here in this bar if I didn't.

My shift was four nights a week, from five P.M. to midnight. This gave Scott time to leave, see his family, take care of a few things, then come back for a few hours and close up at two or three in the morning, depending on how busy it was.

"Your job is to listen to him," Eve had said. "Ply him with booze, get to be his friend, or listen to what he says to other people. Find out his schedule, where he drives to find his revenge, what he plans to do. Then we'll figure out the best night to get him. He hasn't been coming home until five, six in the morning lately, so he must be out there haunting the roads."

Her plan seemed simple enough: once I found out his route, she and I would drive out and wait for him. We would park, I'd open the hood like I was checking the car for a problem. She would wear a wig and a lot of make-up. He would spot her but not know it was her; he would think it was the same people who had hijacked him. He would get out of his car and when he realized she was Eve, his wife, he would get confused, and I would attack him with a baseball bat. We'd leave him there, dead.

"Everyone knows he's been out looking for the people who embarrassed his manhood; the cops will figure he met up with them or someone. He was asking for it."

"And then what?"

"And *then*," she said, pressing her naked body against mine, "it's you and me, darling, and all his money! *And*," she added, "a fat life insurance policy pay-off."

"How fat?"

"One hundred grand, baby."

A hundred g's. Plus what he was worth—bank account,

insurance and finance companies, real estate; Eve figured it was close to three hundred g's.

Any other time I would never have agreed to such a crazy idea, to commit murder; but I was backed up against a wall with Lucy's pregnancy and Kay's demands for more time, to "save" what was left of our marriage. I wanted out. I needed out. I wanted to get far, far away from Hittsville and the state of New York, and I wanted to do it with Eve Fremont.

"We'll go to Europe," she said, "Paris and London and Madrid! We'll travel the world, my darling!"

Sounded good to me. Even if the cops got wise, what could they do to us if we were halfway across the globe?

* * * * * * *

Lucy wasn't happy about my bartending job for two reasons: it kept me away from her some nights and I had an excuse to drink more.

"You said you were going to cut back on the boozing," she reminded me.

"That was because money was getting low," I told her.

"You need to stop drinking so much, Jack," she said, "it's not good for you."

"I know what's good for me," I said, pulling her close, placing my hands on those magnificent young breasts. "Is it my imagination," I asked, "or have these ripe melons gotten bigger?"

"It's because I'm carrying your baby," she said, "that's what happens to women when they have something growing inside of them, the milk starts to churn."

"Oh yeah."

"What do you mean 'oh yeah'? Don't tell me you forgot already!"

"Slipped my mind."

"Or you don't want to be reminded."

"Come here."

"Do you hate our baby?"

"Of course not."

"Do you love the baby?"

"I need to get to know him first."

"Or *her.*"

"Or her."

"It's happened, and now we have to live with it," she said, "and live with it for the rest of our lives. Being a parent is a life-long thing."

"Unless you don't have parents," I said.

"Or bad ones," she said.

"Come here."

"You smell like liquor!"

"So?"

"It makes me want some."

"So let's go get some."

"A woman isn't supposed to drink or smoke when she's with child."

"Who said?"

"I read it."

"Where?"

"I forget."

"What do they know?"

"Sounds like it's the cautious thing to do."

"It's so small and underdeveloped, it's no human being yet," I said, "and if it's half me, booze ain't gonna do any harm. We'll just have a few, okay? Get out of this dump room for awhile and get some air."

She finally agreed. We walked down to the bar on the corner and sat at the counter.

"Rye and two beers," I said.

"Just beer," she said.

"Rye and two beers," I said again.

The bartender shrugged. He looked at Lucy for a moment, then me, then he shrugged again and shook his head and gave us our drinks.

If Lucy walked into a bar alone, they would ask her age,

wonder what a girl so young is doing in a bar. But when she was with me, they never said a word. They just wanted to sell booze, and they figured she must know what she's doing. Maybe she just looked younger than me.

After a few drinks she seemed to loosen up and get randy with me, kissing my face and grabbing me between the legs.

I had to go, I was holding it in. I wasn't gone in the men's bathroom thirty seconds, and I came out and some clown is sitting on my bar stool and trying to make time with my girl.

"C'mon, you can tell me your name at least, honey?" he was saying.

She ignored him.

He had dirty hands, looked like he may have been one of the pipe crew digging out there.

"What the hell," I said, "excuse me, buddy."

He kept his eyes on her. "Take a graze in the grass."

"That's my seat."

"Who says?"

"See that drink on the counter? Belongs to me."

He handed me the drink. "So long."

"It's his seat," Lucy said.

"Not anymore," the joker said.

"You're gonna get me mad," I said.

"I'm trembling in fear. Can't you see I'm busy with the pretty lady here?"

"I see she's pretty as hell," I said, "but looks like she doesn't even know you exist."

"She knows I'm here."

He reached out to touch her and she slapped his hand away.

I laughed.

"I'm a married woman," she said.

"I see no ring," he said.

"This is my husband, Jack," she said.

He looked at me now. "Husband, eh?"

"Yep," I said. "Lucky guy is me."

"Well, married women can become widows fast," he said,

balling his hands into fists.

"Hey," the bartender said, "both of you, nothing in here."

Lucy jumped in my arms. "Baby," she said and kissed me, "let's get out of here, too many rats and insects in this place."

"Good idea."

"Aw, rot," the guy said. "What the hell? What does a gal like that see in a fellow like *him*?"

He had a point, I thought.

"What would any gal see in *you*?" Lucy spat.

"Rot," he said.

We left the bar. We were both walking funny, we were that drunk. We held onto each other, walking back to Wilma's rooming house.

"Men," she said. "Why are all men like that?"

"Not all."

"Most," she said. "Why?"

"Because we're all bastards, we men," I said.

In the room, I showed her what a bastard I could be, I showed her all night, and she didn't complain any.

* * * * * * *

And then there was Kay, my lush tramp wife.

Except, when I came home to get some clean clothes, she didn't appear to be drunk, and she was dressed in a plain blue sack dress.

"Good grief, Jack, where the hell you been?" she said.

I didn't know how long I had been away—perhaps four days. She grabbed me and hugged me.

"I thought something bad happened, Jack! Oh Jack!"

Again, she looked and smelled sober and that was a surprise.

"Nothing bad happened," I said.

"What are you doing, Jack?"

"I need to take a shower, and then I need to get some clothes, and then...."

"And then you're leaving again?"

I nodded.

"Why do you even bother coming home?" she asked. "This isn't 'home' for you, you're hardly here."

"I could say the same."

"I've been home all week."

"Doing what?"

"Getting this place decent is what. Haven't you noticed?"

I looked around. The apartment was spotless—the wood floors shined, there were no beer cans on the floor, empty wine bottles...I glanced in the kitchen and saw the sink porcelain shining, and no dirty dishes.

"Nice," I said.

"I've been working hard."

"I've been working too."

"You found a new job?" she said brightly.

I told her about The Dells.

"That place is a toilet," she said.

"It's a job."

"And you work the late shift?"

"That's why I've been gone," I lied. "By the time I close up, it's three A.M. and I've been drinking some, so I shouldn't drive."

"Where do you sleep?"

I shrugged. "In the car. Or I get a room."

"So why can't you come home during the day?"

"I'm asleep, dammit," I told her, "and when I wake up, it's time to go to work."

"Jack...."

"What are you complaining about, Kay? The rent gets paid here. I go out and work and the rent gets paid and you have a roof over your head, it's not like you're paying anything."

"I was thinking of getting a job."

"Good."

"I'm serious."

"Doing what?"

"Anything," she said. "Diner, factory...I can work."

"But can you work sober?"

"Jack, I haven't been drinking. Can't you tell?"

"Look, I need a shower," I said. "Let me get the sweat and grime off me and then we can talk, okay?"

She nodded. "Talking would be nice."

Three minutes later, my head under the nozzle, I felt hands on me, a body against my body.

Kay had joined me.

"Kay," I said, "what are you doing?"

"Can't a wife bathe with her husband?"

"Look," I said.

"What?" she said, grabbing me below.

She kissed me.

I responded.

We kissed.

"I know what you *like*, I know what you *need*," my tramp wife said.

I didn't need it, but I liked it.

Perhaps she needed it.

* * * * * * *

Eve wanted it and needed it at the hotel room that night, and I did the best I could and was surprised I had any energy left after the session I had with Kay. A man does what he has to do.

She was more interested in her husband's visits to the bar.

"I just started, and he's been in once, for a short while," I told her, "and then he said he had business on the road."

"Looking for those people who shamed him," Eve said. She shook her head. "The ego of that man."

"Eve, tell me."

"Tell you what?"

"You know what."

"Oh, Jack, please."

"How often?"

"Why do you want to know?"

"I just do."

"Do I ask you how often you make love to your wife?"

I just did, I wanted to say.

"Do you want to know?" I said.

"No," she said, "why would I?"

"Curiosity."

"Didn't you hear?"

"Hear?"

"It killed the cat. Now shut up," and she grabbed me, kissed me, demanded me.

I gave her what she wanted.

And I gave it to her again.

Then I went to work.

5.

Scott looked haggard. He was glad I was taking the late shift over from him. He was drunk, too, drinking shots and beer with customers, and I could tell something was wrong. I asked him about it.

"Does it show?" he said.

"It shows," I said.

"Look, I'm married. My wife, I love her," he said, pouring himself a shot of rye. "But things happen. There's this little sweetheart, she used to come in here, but I fell something bad for her." He poured himself another shot. "Twenty-two years old. What's a man like me think he can do with a young lady? But I did, and she did, and now she thinks she's in a family way."

"Thinks?"

"You know how women are."

I nodded.

"You ever knock a girl up?"

I shook my head. I didn't want to tell him about Lucy. He didn't need to know anything about my life, and I had to keep up the charade as Eve Fremont's cousin.

"Lucky," he said.

"You have kids?"

"Two, one in college and one married with her own kids. My wife and I—we married at sixteen, with the first kid. I'm an old guy, do I need a new baby?"

"There are ways to, you know."

"That's what I told her. She said no. She said she wouldn't kill the baby. She says she wants it, if it's true. She goes to see the doc tomorrow. It's my wife that worries me the most. How will *she* take it? This is something I can't keep from her, after all. Or can I?"

"Does she need to know?" I asked.

"True," Scott said. "We all have our dark secrets, eh?"

* * * * * * *

Paul Fremont came in that night and he stayed for five hours, and the more he drank, the more his mouth spouted out garbage. Every minute he got louder and louder.

I didn't like him, and not only because he was married to Eve. He was simply a drunk old man who was full of himself, a man with money who looked down on everyone around him. A man with quite an ego. Now I knew what Eve was talking about, how his ego was injured and his need for revenge.

"I'll get them," he said now and then, more to himself, talking into his beer or a shot of vodka. "I'll get those bastards and that bitch and I'll show them. I know they're out there. I can feel them. I can smell them. They'll try it again, but this time I'll give them quite the surprise, and they'll have dinner in hell, I tell you."

He liked to talk to the b-girls that wandered in and hung around. I had a feeling he'd slept with them all at one time or another. They all knew he had money and plenty of it.

"He's not very good in the sack," I heard one girl say to another girl while Fremont was in the bathroom.

"Does it matter as long as he pays?" the other girl said

"I guess not. But it's not always the money. You wanna have fun too, and get paid, have the best of both worlds."

"I hear you, sister."

Fremont returned and ordered a double shot of vodka and a mug of beer. He was weaving around. Another man, I might have cut him off, but I didn't care how much Fremont drank or what kind of trouble he might get himself into.

"You wanna know what the trouble with tramps is?" he said to me.

"Sure," I said.

A good bartender always listens.

"A tramp is always a tramp," he told me. "They try to fool you, they may even fool themselves. They think they've changed and maybe they want to; they say it's all behind in the past, but deep down, down in their rotten cores, they're still tramps. They are born tramps and will die tramps. Like those harlots there," and he nodded at three b-girls talking among themselves. "They've grown up in the slums and this is the only life they know. Their mothers were probably whores, and they probably don't even know who their daddies are, some fellah their whore mothers met at a bar, maybe this bar. This rat hole has been around long enough."

He drank, brooding.

"A tramp is a tramp, like my damn wife."

Now I was listening.

"Thought maybe I married a gal who had changed her sinful ways, but she's no different than she was five years ago when she was modeling for nudie photos. You ever seen those pictures, of women?"

"Now and then."

"What do you think?"

I shrugged. "Where there's a demand, someone will provide it."

"Not that I care much," he said. "She was nineteen at the time. I married a girl half my age, you know."

"I didn't know."

"I'm man enough for her, but sometimes I wonder if she's stepping out on me, you know. What do you think?"

I started to worry that he was testing me; that he wasn't as drunk as he was acting and knew more than I realized.

"Could be my imagination," he said. "I'm just thinking lately that she hasn't changed none. You know how I met her?"

"No."

"In New York. She was working a convention I was at. You know what a convention girl is, right?"

"Heard of them."

"They call them 'hostesses,' but they're just whores, hookers, and tramps out for a buck, higher class than the trash in here, but a whore is a whore no matter what clothes you put her in. So I paid for her, you know, she's pretty, why not, and she gives me this song and dance about how she hates what she does, how she has no choice, she can't get a decent job in the city because she never went to college or even graduated high school, how she wants to find the right man and settle down and maybe even have a kid or two. Ah, she played this old man good. Give me another hit, buddy."

I poured more vodka.

"Played right into my lonely old heart. Tells me age doesn't matter. A month later, I'm married to her."

"That's quite a story," I said.

"Married to a tramp," he said.

It wasn't easy to keep my emotions inside. I wanted to punch his teeth out, I wanted him on the ground, and I wanted to kick him in the guts and the groin. He was talking about the woman I loved: his wife.

No man should speak of his wife that way.

I'm a hypocrite.

I have talked that way about my own wife.

Kay, the lush and the whore.

* * * * * * *

I thought about everything Paul Fremont said that night. "Tramps never change, no matter how much they try to convince you." Was this true for Kay? She told me she had quit drinking, that she went to group meetings now, that she wasn't bringing strange men home from the bars. That afternoon, after we made love, she said she was turning a new leaf and wanted our marriage to work. I went along with her, only half-listened to her. I had other things on my mind.

I had the blonde on my mind.

Eve.

Eve Fremont, convention girl.

When Eve and I got together the next day, she could tell something was wrong with me.

"You seem distant," she said.

"Just thinking."

"About what?"

"This and that."

"Tell me about my husband last night."

"Do you have to call him that?"

"Sorry," she said. "Tell me about Paul, what was he like last night at the bar?"

I told her.

"Typical."

Then I told her more: what he said about her.

"Now I know why you're acting odd," she said. She got up, went to the bathroom.

I stayed on the bed, naked, waiting for her.

She came out, lighted a cigarette, and leaned against the hotel room wall.

"I won't lie to you, Jack," she said. "What he said is true. I was working a convention in Philly when I met him."

"He said New York."

"It was Philadelphia. He was drunk; do you think he remembers where he meets whores?"

"Were you?"

"Was I what? Say it."

"A whore."

"I never sold what's between my legs for money," she said defiantly, angry. "Other girls did, sure. But not every convention girl is a hooker. We get paid by agencies to talk to and be nice to men coming in from out of town. The men buy us drinks, dinner, sometimes they offer to pay for alone time in bed. I won't say it was all morals, that I wasn't cheap—I just didn't find those men attractive. Not like you. They're all old, fat, balding, smell like cigars, they think they're the bees knees with their money and their accounts and the people they know, but to me they were just dirty old men."

"Like Paul Fremont."

"He gave me a sob story. About his wife who died of cancer. It *was* a sad story, you know. And he said he had all this wealth, money, stocks, real estate, and nobody to leave it to—no wife, no kids. And he asked me to marry him."

"And you said yes."

"You know that."

I nodded.

She came to me, sat on the bed and touched my leg.

"Jack, I've been honest with you," Eve said. "I don't fit the rich woman role well, but I like it. I like money. I said that from the start. I like the comfort and security it brings. You have no idea how I grew up, how poor my family was. Sometimes things got so bad that my father picked food out of the trash. You don't know that kind of poverty."

I thought of the world Lucy came from.

"I know it," I said. "I didn't come from any great beginnings. My folks were always broke, in hock—and look at me now: I barely have two nickels to rub together."

She smiled, her hand moving up my leg. "The day is coming soon, darling, when all that will change. You will never be broke again. We'll spend Paul's money and spit on his grave and laugh and make love and laugh and make love and be happy."

"Will we?"

"Do you believe me?"

"I can believe anything."

Even if I lived to a hundred years old, I would never have the kind of wealth Paul Fremont had. Sure, I hated him just for that, and I hated him for the way he talked about Eve, and the way he carried himself in the bar, like he was above everyone, like he was some giant and we were all ants he could squish under his shoe.

"He has to have everything, doesn't he?" I said.

"He's used to getting what he wants. He's used to winning. That's why his getting robbed like that has him all twisted up. His ego will be his downfall."

"We have to be sensible about this, Eve."

"My plan will work, and then I will be free from him."

"He got you," I pointed out. "He saw you and he got you. Nearly sixty years old and he owns your twenty-four-year-old body."

"You're wrong. He doesn't own me. He's just renting it, and I am going to evict him from it."

"Who does own it, Eve?"

She lay down on top of me. "You can, if you desire. I will be all yours body and soul."

"Let's go over your plan again."

"Later. There's something else we have to do."

And we did it.

And we did it again.

Then we went over her plan.

* * * * * * *

He was out there every night, hunting for the bank robbers from Syracuse who had made a fool of him. As if they were still around these parts, as if they would risk doing it again. But Paul Fremont was not thinking straight.

From my observations at the bar, he always left around one in the morning, when he was well tanked up and feeling ballsy. Eve said he was coming home every night around four and five.

That meant he was prowling the outer roads three to four hours each night.

We would do it in two nights. I had that one off from the bar.

I was nervous, but her plan seemed sound enough to work, crazy as it was. Who would ever suspect?

During the daytime hours of the day in question, I went to see Roger, in case things went wrong and I never saw him again. We had some beers and he said he was almost done with his peeping tom novel, in which case he could stop doing his "research."

"Cripes," I said, "you told me you were gonna stop prowling."

"I cut back."

"You're gonna get yourself tossed in jail."

Look at me: I was going to murder a man tonight, and I was giving him advice about keeping out of legal trouble.

"I'm touched about your concern," he said, "but I'm *very* careful."

Eve and I would be careful too.

I went to see Kay, but she wasn't there. In the kitchen I found a dozen empty beer cans and an empty bottle of tequila.

She quit.

Sure.

People never change.

And then there was Lucy.

"You're gone too much, Jack," she complained.

"Working."

"The bar, I know."

"I have to."

"Can't you find a job during the day, so we will have more nights to be together, instead of sleeping?"

I had been sleeping at the room more than home, and I had never spent a night with Eve. Here, with Lucy, I came home and fell asleep, and she got up early to go to the diner.

Every morning, she'd look at herself in the mirror and say, "Am I showing yet?"

She'd ask that if I was awake or asleep.

I pretended to be asleep because I didn't want to deal with the issue.

I guess you can say I was in denial about the whole baby growing inside her. I had other things on my mind.

And I felt bad about what I intended to do. I was going to leave her once Eve was free. I had no idea where Eve and I would go—we'd talked about California or Nevada—but it would be far away from Hittsville.

I vowed I'd make it right. I would send her money, I would take care of the baby, just not here and as a husband.

I couldn't do it.

As for Kay...well, that was another thing.

One thing after the other.

6.

Eve wore a long black wig that covered half her face, this way her husband would not recognize her when he flashed his headlights on the girl—plus the girl who was with the men who took him down had black hair, so in his drunken rage of revenge he would think this was the same girl.

She looked good as a dark brunette. I almost wanted to take her and pretend she was someone else.

We took my car, parked it on the side of the road. I lifted the hood, to make it seem there was something wrong with the engine.

Eve also provided the baseball bat.

"As he comes toward me, you rush and crack him in the skull," she said, "and do it hard. If you don't have the guts to cave his brains in, you just give me the bat and I'll take care of business. All I want you to do is knock him down, knock him out."

"You really think this will work?"

"There are plenty of witnesses who know he's driving around all night looking for trouble. He talks about it at the bar. The cops will figure he found his trouble, maybe even the same folks who got him before. They'll pin the murder rap on them—what the heck, you know, they're already guilty for one killing, and they did that bank robbery, they're going to get the chair either way."

"Or life."

"I'd rather have the chair," Eve said, "who wants to rot away in prison forever, every day playing in your mind what you could have done different to be free, white, and twenty-one."

You just might get that wish, I thought. The both of us.

I had to agree: I'd want the electric chair over life.

Hell, the firing squad.

She must have seen the uncertainty on my face.

"Come here, lover," and she pulled me toward her. "What can momma do to make you feel better?"

"Go get a room and some rye and...," I started to say.

"Hush," and she put her fingers to my lips. "In due time. We have to work for that heaven. Nothing in this crazy life comes easy and without a price."

"A price too high."

"But a gift well worth it."

She kissed me.

I held her.

"Tell me this will work without a hitch," I said.

"It has to," she said. "What other way could there be? I don't want to stay married to that pig another day."

I thought about Kay. I wanted to be free from her, too. I thought about Lucy, and I didn't know what the hell I was going to do with her; I'd deal with her and the flesh growing inside her later on.

"Someone is coming!" Eve said, excitement and fear in her voice.

There was indeed a set of headlights about half a mile away. The land was flat, the night was dark, you could see a car a mile away.

"Positions!" Eve said.

I went to the other side of the road and crouched behind some shrubs, baseball bat in hand. Eve stood by the car.

What do you think about when you're waiting to kill someone? It's easy to answer. You just think about doing the job and having it over with. And you think of the future, a future loaded with money and a woman who knows how to give you what you want and need.

* * * * * * *

"Make me a baby," she goes.

"Hell, I did my best," you go.

"Do it again," she goes.

You do it again and again and again and again, and after awhile it's the world, all of the world. You're lost in her love-liness, lost, and when she says things like that you think of tomorrow. You think of a hundred thousand dollars, or more, a half a million, a million, the spoils of another man's greed and swindles, and you know that there will never be a need to worry. You'll have her and the money and somehow, some way, you will wash the crime of murder out of your blood, out of your life, and there will be no guilt, it will be forgotten.

"I want him to look like you, Jack."

"Or her."

"Her."

"She'll look like you."

"What's the matter as long as it's us?"

* * * * * * *

Lucy and I would never have that worry-free conversation.

The car—a Ford station wagon—slowed down, seeing Eve standing there. I tightened my grip on the bat. The car stopped.

The driver was not her husband.

The driver was a man in his forties, his hair thinning, his crooked teeth prominent. He wore an old tan suit and his eyes bulged at the sight of Eve's shapely shape.

The Ford stopped.

"Car trouble?" the man said, and started to open his door.

"Uh, no," Eve said, "no, not at all."

"Looks to me—"

I dropped the bat and quickly ran across the road.

"Got my business done," I said.

The man looked at me and he was not happy.

"Hey, buddy," I said.

"Hello."

I winked. "Too much beer and nature calls, if you know what I mean."

"Yeah, I do. Your car okay?"

"Sure," I said, walking over to it and dropping the hood. "Just checking the oil. Engine seemed to be running a little hot."

"Yeah, that happens," the man said, looking at Eve and sighing. He was obviously not happy that he wasn't going to get a chance to help this dark-haired beauty and perhaps make her.

"Let's go, darling, we have a long drive ahead of us," I told Eve, and to the man, "Good night, buddy."

"Good night, Mister," Eve said with a smile.

I held the door open for her and she got in.

I went around to the driver's side. The man drove his Ford away fast, tires screeching.

I stopped shaking. Sweat was in my eyes.

"Goddamn it," Eve said.

"It was bound to happen."

"The next one will be him," she said, "I *know* it. I can feel him out there, driving this way."

We sat there, quiet in the dark cold night, and didn't speak. There was nothing to say. I almost suggested we wait for another time, since the fellow in the Ford had seen us. I knew she would not go for it, though.

Twenty minutes passed, and then we spotted another set of lights coming our way.

"It's him," she said.

"Hope so."

"I know so."

"It could be him."

"Positions!"

I walked back across the road to the shrubs and the bat.

You think of the girl back in the room, carrying your child, and what kind of future you have, a father with responsibilities, always broke, going from job to job, no future, no money, and you hate that future. That is not the future you want.

The car was close.

It was a Ford station wagon.

Wasn't Paul driving his Caddy?

Something wasn't right here.

Eve had a leg stuck out, her face turned down, the wig covering her eyes. Before I could warn it, it was too late— two men and a woman jumped out of the Ford, whooping and hollering and laughing.

They were young, late teens or early twenties. The girl held a bottle of rye in her hand. I could tell they were all drunk and out to raise some hell.

They grabbed Eve before she could realize that this was not her husband stopping to help out a lady in distress. Still, she was in distress, in danger, and she screamed as the two hell-bound young men grabbed her and pushed her down.

The young woman poured some rye on Eve's face.

"We're gonna have a party with you!" said the young woman.

The two men laughed.

All this was happening as I rushed them, the baseball bat high up in the air.

The young woman saw me first. She cried out, "Hey, man!" and threw the bottle of rye at my face. I ducked, swung, and hit her in the face with the bat. I didn't care that she was a girl because she was no helpless girl, and I could see it clearly in her eyes: she was evil and mad for kicks and she had killed before.

Killers have certain kinds of eyes you cannot mistake. I'd seen them before, I'd seen the eyes of dangerous animals that pretended to be humans, and I saw it in the girl and I saw it in the eyes of her two companions.

So I had no misgivings when the girl's face exploded into blood and flying teeth and she went down to the ground.

Next: the men....

I got one in the face twice, and down on his skull, and he went down in a bloody mess, hut the other one pulled out a gun and fired three times—missing once, but getting one bullet in my shoulder and one in my arm.

Eve grabbed him by the leg and screamed; she made a sound of fear and anger I'd never heard come from a woman. She bit him on the calf.

The man cried out in pain and pointed the gun at her. He fired but it was a bad aim and he missed her, just barely, as the bullet whizzed past Eve's cheek and impacted on the ground.

This was enough time for me to swing the bat with my uninjured arm at him. I got him, but he got another bullet off, this one grazing my neck. Half an inch to the right and I would have had it in the jugular vein.

I pounded his face into a pulp with the bat.

His body was on the ground, but his skull and face were so caved in that no one would've ever recognized him.

I fell to my knees.

I was crying, surrounded in blood.

My blood, their blood....

Flesh and bone....

Brain matter on the ground, on my shirt and skin....

Teeth everywhere.

Eve was on her feet and she was acting very strange. She was pacing around in a circle and mumbling.

I looked at all the carnage I had created and said, "Cripes," as things started to get dizzy.

I was losing blood, fast, from my shoulder and arm and where I'd been nicked in the neck.

I fell to the ground and everything went predictably black.

7.

You may have read about it in the papers or heard it on the radio. It was the biggest news to ever hit Hittsville.

The three kids were dubbed the "Mad for Kicks Gang," and their combined ages were barely sixty. They were what people called "beatniks," and allegedly hopped up on booze, reefer, and something called "bennies." There was mention of heroin. They had robbed that bank in Syracuse, they had robbed Paul Fremont and others for cars, taking a new car every day to thwart off the police, and they had killed some people, raped some women, and castrated a man "for the kicks."

That's what they wanted with Eve—they must have thought what luck, a woman stranded in a broken-down car, the same ruse they used. They would have defiled Eve, perhaps even killed her, and taken off with the car. They didn't expect me, however, they had no idea that we had planned our own crime.

So I was a hero. I had killed the killers.

Oh, the cops and the district attorney were none too happy with my homicidal spree, but it was self-defense, and these Mad for Kicks kids were pretty homicidal themselves.

"Did you have to pound that one's face in so badly?"

"Yes, I did," I said. "I was shot. I didn't stop to think about it."

There was no chance that I would be charged with murder, not when the town saw me as a hero and the bank in Syracuse offered me a reward of $1,000. The money the kids had stolen was mostly recovered, except for $3,000 of it.

I guess they found some packets of heroin in their car with the money, nestled in the back of the station wagon in a milk crate.

* * * * * * *

My stay in the hospital wasn't too bad, despite the discomfort. They gave me good drugs for the pain. The doctors told me I was lucky no major arteries had been hit. Nurses tended to me, and they were all attractive and sweet and called me "hero." The newspaper reporters interviewed me, but I told them very little, told them I just got lucky, and was happy I was not dead.

I'd lost four pints of blood by the time an ambulance got out there. Apparently, Eve had flagged down a passing car and she was taken to a phone booth. "A good Samaritan called it in," the police told me, "but we don't know her name."

That was my cue.

I may have been injured badly, but I was not stupid.

The cops had no idea Eve was there. The only witnesses were dead and they'd never talk.

This means I didn't have to explain why I was out in the middle of a dark road with another man's wife, said man having been a victim of the Mad for Kicks gang.

As far as the police were concerned, I had been driving alone and had some car trouble and met up with the Mad for Kicks crew, and, having heard about them, reached for my bat as they came after me.

It was a good story that they had deduced, and I went along with it.

But what happened to Eve?

* * * * * * *

Kay came to visit me twice. She was quiet and almost shell-shocked, as if she didn't believe this was happening.

I knew how she felt.

Both times, she asked, "How are you feeling, Jack?"

Both times, I replied, "Like dog crap that someone stepped on and then wiped on the side of the pavement. Other than that, not too shabby, as long as the drugs keep coming and keep me in the clouds."

She told me some reporters were bothering her, from the local paper, from Syracuse, even one from New York.

I told her not to talk to them if she didn't want to.

On her second visit, she said, "Jack, I need to ask you something."

"Okay."

"A few things."

"Go ahead."

"What were you doing out there on the road that late at night?"

"Car trouble," I said.

"That's what I'm told, but...."

"But what?"

"Nothing," she said.

"Something is on your mind."

She said, "The reporters...."

"They still bugging you?"

"Not anymore. But they said...they asked me...they told me...."

"What? Spill it, woman."

"They asked me about another woman," Kay said. "That you had some woman—a girl—in a rooming house and she was pregnant."

I didn't know what to say to that.

Lucy. Lucy had not come to visit me. I hadn't called her, talked to her, because I didn't want anyone—the cops, the reporters, the nurses—to know about her. I didn't want that news to spread for this exact reason.

"Jack?"

"And you believe what you heard?"

"I don't know."

"You know how they like to make things up, these damn reporters."

She just looked at me.

"Say it, Kay," I told her.

She said, "They told me her name. Lucy. They told me where she lived. So I went to where they told me, to see if she was real, to—talk to her."

"Talk to an imaginary person?" I said, and laughed.

"Stop lying to me, Jack. I went there but she wasn't there. An old woman, this woman named Wilma, said the girl had left. Moved out. And in a hurry. But this Wilma knew you, Jack. She knew you well. She said you were around often and usually paid the rent. She knew all about you, too, she reads the papers, she thinks you're some big hero like everyone else."

I closed my eyes.

There was no sense in lying.

"Okay," I said, "it's true."

"I know it's true," she said. "I'm not mad. Why should I be? Considering all that I've done...."

I opened my eyes.

I said, "All the whoring around."

"Yes, I whored around."

"All the drinking."

"I drank too much."

"You're a tramp," I told her, "a slut and a whore and lush. So, yes, I had another woman, I had a lover, and I love her, and yes, she's having my child, and you have no call to say anything bad about it."

"I know," she said, nodding, "but it's not fair, Jack."

"What's not fair? After all the men you've—"

"Not that. Not that. I mean, the baby she's carrying. It's not fair."

"Not fair," I said.

"That you gave her a baby, but I can't have a baby."

"It's a blessing you never got pregnant," I said, "the way you carry on. What kind of life, what kind of mother would you be for a kid?"

"I told you I've changed, Jack! Didn't you see? Weren't you listening? I stopped the drinking. I've gone to A.A. meetings. I've cleaned myself up. I...I've even got myself a job."

"Really. A job?"

"It's part-time. At this diner...the same diner where your Lucy worked. Since she left, they needed someone, so I took that job."

"Where is she?"

"Lucy?"

"Where is she?"

"How would I know? She was gone when I went looking for her...."

"Did you do something, Kay? Tell me the truth."

"I'm telling you honest," she said. "The girl was gone. She's gone. She has your kid growing in her belly and she's gone, doesn't that worry you?"

"Of course it worries me," I said, not sure if it did. "But what the hell can I do when I'm holed up here?"

"It's not fair, Jack."

"So it's not fair."

I had to consider this—if Lucy left, wherever she went, and never came back, I wouldn't have to deal with the pregnancy and raising a kid, or what the law might say about her age. I'd be free. I could divorce Kay, and Eve could leave her husband, and Eve and I....

Eve and me.

Were there still an Eve and Jack? Was there that possibility now, and the money, and all the future days of beer, booze, sex, and leisure?

Kay was at the door.

"When can you leave here?" she asked.

"Soon, I hope."

"I guess we have a lot of talking to do later."

"I don't know. Do we?"

"I hope so."

"What is there to talk about?"

"Our marriage."

"There's no more marriage, Kay."

"Don't say that."

"Even after you know, about Lucy and the baby?"

"I have no hate about that, Jack. And I think we can save our marriage. I hope we can."

"I don't know, Kay."

"Will you come home when you get out?"

"I don't know," I said.

I didn't know anything right now.

* * * * * * *

My next visitor was one I didn't expect, and one I dreaded.

My heart jumped into my neck when he walked into the hospital room.

Paul Fremont.

He wore a pale blue suit and hat. He took off his hat. His hair was matted in sweat. It was a hot day out there.

"Good day, Jack Card."

"Good day...Mr. Fremont," I said.

"Paul."

"Paul."

"May I call you Jack?"

"It's my name, sir."

"Don't 'sir' me, okay?"

"Sure."

"How they been treating you here?"

"Very well."

"Those nurses are lookers."

"Some are."

"And they've given you the good stuff to keep the pain away?"

"Very good."

"And you have your very own private room, one of the best." He looked around. "Yes, the best room this establishment has."

"It is a fine room." I said cautiously.

"It better be, for what I've been paying." He smiled. "That's right, Jack, I've been footing your hospital bill."

I had wondered about that, but was afraid to ask. I figured maybe the police or the city or the bank in Syracuse was, or that perhaps I'd be presented with a bill at some time, and it'd come out of my $1,000 reward.

Now, I was told, Paul Fremont, the man I hated because he

was married to the woman I desired, the man I had planned to murder, was my benefactor.

He turned and looked out the window, playing with his hat in one hand.

He asked, "Do you know why I've been paying your bill, Jack?"

"No," I said.

"Well, wouldn't you say it's the least I could do? You killed those three creep kids who robbed me. Granted, I wanted to do it myself, but so be it, revenge was taken care of. You did me a solid favor, so this was the least I could do."

"Well...thank you for that," I said.

"But it's funny, wouldn't you say?"

"I'm not sure."

"Well, that here you are, you once painted my house, and then you were working in the bar I own, and you just happen to cross paths with these Mad for Kicks creeps."

"Getting shot isn't funny," I said.

"No, no, of course not." He turned around and looked at me, coldly. "What is funny is you and my wife."

I couldn't look at him.

"Eve," he said. "You know my wife, Eve."

"I know who she is, but I don't know her."

"Look here, Jack. Let's cut the crap. I know about you and Eve."

"What do you think you know, Paul?"

"I had her followed. Weeks ago. I knew what she was up to, but I didn't know with whom. And then I find out. And then you're working at the bar. Funny, isn't it?"

"You're not laughing."

"Not anymore."

"What do you want, Paul?"

"I want you to keep seeing her," he said. "Do what you were doing before. Sleep with the tramp. I don't care. I need to divorce her. But I don't want her to take a goddamn dime of my money. If I prove that she was unfaithful, that she was cheating on me, then the court won't grant her a penny. Oh, I may give her a dollar—imagine the look on her face, I hand her one dollar as I boot her fanny out of my house."

This time he did laugh.

I did not find him funny.

"Pictures are good, but testimony is rock solid, so says my attorney. I hear the bank gave you a reward, yes?"

"Yes."

"A grand, huh? Not bad. How would you like five more?"

"What?"

"Five thousand dollars for your testimony in court," he said. "You tell the judge all about your sordid affair with my wife—details, times, dates, places, what she did to you in bed and what you did to her. For that, you get five grand."

Five. Six thousand dollars total. I couldn't make that in two years worth of labor. I could start a new life, somewhere far away.

Far away and alone? Without Eve....

Or with her. She could go along with it. We'd start a new life together with six grand and work on getting more. Start a business somewhere....

I looked Paul Fremont in the eye. Yes he knew about my affair with his wife, and he didn't care about that. I also knew he had no idea that she had plotted his murder and I was in on it.

Everyone believed my encounter with the Mad for Kicks kids was simple fate and odd luck.

"I need to think about it," I told him.

"Think on it, but don't take long," he said, "because the next thing you know, your bills are no longer being paid and the hospital kicks you out. And maybe the police start asking funny questions about that night, eh?"

Maybe he did know, or suspected.

"Give me a day," I said.

He started for the door, and then stopped.

"You're not the only one, Jack. You know that, right?"

"Know what?"

"She's cheated on me with other men, men like you, before. Started less than a month after I married the whore. I told you what she was. I told you that night at the bar. I was drunk, but I was telling you for a reason, because I already knew then about you and her. I was warning you. And I'm warning you now. She may have promised you things, but they're all lies. You're thinking, okay, she divorces Paul Fremont, and she's clear to be with you. She might be with you for awhile, Jack, but sooner or later she'll betray you. It's in her nature, it's what she is: a worthless tramp. I told you what she was when I met her. That's never changed. She'll always be a whore at heart to the day she becomes a little old woman and dies at age ninety. If she ever lives that long."

He started for the door, and stopped again.

"Oh, I have a gift for you too, something to help you think faster about what I asked."

He left.

Two minutes later, one of the nurses walked in. She was the best of them, tall with red hair and a good thirty-eight-inch bust.

"Hello, there, Jack," she said.

There was something odd about the way she said that, her voice deep and low.

"Hi...Libby, right?"

"Libby the Sinner," she said, coming to me.

"Libby Sin," I said.

She unzipped the front of her uniform, showing me what she had. She wasn't wearing a bra.

"Do you like?" she asked.

"I'd be dead if I said no."

She climbed into the bed with me, sitting on top of me.

"What are you doing?" I said.

"You don't want me to?"

"I didn't say that."

"Be quiet and enjoy this. Mr. Fremont paid top dollar."

My gift.

He was right—they were all whores, all had for a price.

"He paid for you to have a good time," Libby the nurse said, "and I'm going to show you the best time."

She did.

We did.

All the rest of that day, and into the night.

No one bothered us.

We rested between bouts and went at it again and again.

"Am I good?" she asked.

"The best," I said.

"I might've even done it free. Who doesn't want to love a hero?"

She showed me what she felt about heroes again.

It was almost morning when she finally left and I went to sleep, thinking about the six thousand dollars.

8.

A candy striper entered my room later that morning, acting clandestine about it. She was a cute young thing with strawberry blonde hair, no more than fifteen. I couldn't believe that Fremont had hired her, and I wondered if I had anything left in me after last night, but here I was being a dirty old man. The girl was not here for sex.

"I have a message for you," she said, almost a whisper, handing me a folded sheet of paper.

"A message?"

"From Eve," she said with a wink.

I thanked her and the girl left.

I almost wished she would've stayed. But did I need the trouble, another underaged girl?

I unfolded the piece of paper. In Eve's neat handwriting:

My Dear Jack,

I can't risk coming to the hospital to see you. People would talk and Paul is acting very strange, like he knows something. Please find a way to get out of there and meet me at our special place at our usual time.

Love always—Your Eve

Our special place was that room of sin in the hotel of lust.

How the hell was I suppose to get out of here? I hadn't been discharged. But—I wasn't a prisoner here, either. I could come or go as I please, couldn't I?

The usual time was six o'clock. I still had all day to rest and think of the best way to slip out of the hospital unnoticed.

I napped.

I had lunch.

I napped some more.

At four, the night shift of nurses came on. I would use the bustle of the changeover to make my escape.

It hurt to get out of bed. It hurt to put my clothes on. My whole body ached and the two entry points where bullets had been screamed bloody agony when I slipped on my jeans and put on my shirt.

What the hell; I was going to live with this pain one way or another for the rest of my life. This was the price I had to pay for wanting money and a woman named Eve.

The perfect woman.

The perfect hell.

The perfect drug.

* * * * * * *

Getting out was easier than I anticipated. I just left my room while no one was around or looking, waltzed down the hall to the fire exit, opened the door, and there I was, on the first floor, out in the world, the sun setting, the day ending, and the night taking over.

There was a cabstand by the hospital and I jumped into a taxi and told the driver where to take me.

"You got it."

I was early.

The desk clerk who knew me well said Eve had not checked in yet. He gave me the key to our usual room anyway. "I can trust a hero," he said. Sometimes being a hero in other people's eyes has its advantages.

I waited in the room.

And waited.

And waited.

She did not arrive at six, at seven, or eight.

Or nine.

Something wasn't right.

Something was wrong.

I couldn't call her.

I didn't know what to do.

I didn't feel like waiting any longer, and I didn't want to stay here all night alone.

I didn't know, at that moment, what had happened to Eve, what she had done, and I wouldn't know until the next day. Had I known, I would've taken my $1,000 and hauled tail out of town. I wouldn't have had to deal with the aftermath of the shock, or the aftermath of the surprise that I was to find at my apartment, or the shock of what Roger Weaver did.

A lot of bad stuff went down that night.

Maybe I should've stayed at the hospital.

* * * * * * *

First, I went home to get my clothes. I needed clean clothes, more clothes than what I had on my back. I hoped Kay wasn't there so I wouldn't have to deal with her, her questions, her oaths that she had changed and that we could save our marriage.

It was night and any other time she'd be down at the bars talking men into buying her beer or shots of rye.

I saw a light on in the apartment, and I heard voices, some laughter—hers, and a man's.

She had changed her wanton ways—my foot!

I should have burst in there, caught her surprised, ridiculed her, but I decided to casually stroll in and cleared my throat to get her attention.

Kay screamed, grabbed her blouse on the floor, and covered herself. She was topless, wearing only panties and a garter.

The man with her held a camera, and he was taking photos of her. He stopped when Kay piped out her surprise, and turned around to look at me.

"You," he said.

"I'll be damned," I said.

It was Jed, all stocky five feet of him, and the bastard was taking lewd photos of my wife.

"What are you doing here?" he asked.

"What are you doing in my place, with my wife?"

Jed laughed quite heartily. "Wife? *Wife?!* Now ain't that something. What happened to your teen chippie?"

That was it. I may have been in pain but I could take Jed out and that's just what I did. He'd had this coming for awhile.

I swung.

He got it in the face.

The camera fell on the floor and broke.

"You're gonna pay!" Jed yelled.

He came after me but it was a mistake; I had too much youth, energy, anger and experience over him.

I really gave him a pounding. A lot of his teeth were on the floor.

Kay cried for me to stop. "You're going to kill him, Jack!"

She jumped on my back.

"Stop, Jack, stop!"

I pushed her away and looked down at Jed. He was going to be in for some pain and hell when he woke up.

I said to Kay, "What the hell were you doing with this joker?"

"Just what it looked like," she answered defiantly.

"Photos?"

"I need money, Jack!"

"What about the job?"

"Like that pays anything."

"Why him? Do you know who *he is*? Where did you meet him?"

"At the bar."

"How surprising."

"He told me—how I could earn some extra money."

"Right."

I went into the bedroom to get some clothes.

She followed me.

"It's not what you're thinking, Jack," she said helplessly.

"I'm not thinking anything," I said.

"I never slept with him."

"That's a first."

"I'm not lying."

"I don't care."

"What are you doing, Jack?"

I was packing all my clothes into a duffle bag.

"Exactly what it looks like," I said.

"Looks like you're leaving," she said.

"Bingo," I said.

"Are you leaving me?"

"Have fun with your new modeling career," I told her.

"Jack! Come back! Please!"

I never intended to return.

9.

I wasn't prepared for what transpired the next day. It was in the newspaper, and people all over town were talking about it: Paul Fremont was dead. His young wife had killed him with a gun they had in their home. She was in jail and claiming that it was self-defense, that he wouldn't let her leave the house and he threatened to murder her, so she took action. Didn't sound like the cops believed her story; Fremont was a pillar of the community, a rich man with influence, and everyone knew she was a wild wanton.

My name did not pop up, at least not in the newspapers. I wondered how long it would take the cops to put a few things together and come talk to me. Unless Mrs. Fremont started to talk about lovers and murder plots.

In a smaller front-page story, bottom right-hand corner, was this headline:

PEEPING TOM CAUGHT IN THE ACT!

The peeping tom, the article stated, was a reclusive writer of trashy paperbacks, one Roger Weaver.

* * * * * * *

"You shouldn't have come here, kid," said Roger Weaver from behind the glass partition.

"I had to."

"I know. But you shouldn't have."

"I'm here," I said.

"Don't you have enough troubles of your own?" he asked.

I shrugged and said, "What's a little more?"

There we sat, in the visitor's area inside the sheriff's holding cell.

"Not getting any gruff?" he said.

"They still think I'm a hero."

"Better than being the villain."

"They're gonna unmask me soon," I said.

"That woman...."

I gave him a look.

"I heard," he said.

"So has everyone."

"No trouble?"

"Like I said...."

"Hero."

I asked, "Roger, why?"

"I told you."

"Don't give me this research crap."

"The book is done."

"Then *why*?"

"I got hooked.... Actually, I'm glad you did come by. You have to do something for me—a dead man's request, a final favor."

"No one is going to kill you."

"You never know, once they send me to the pen downstate. How are peepers treated in gen pop? I'll find out."

"I'll find you a damn good lawyer," I told him.

"I'm not getting out of this one, kid. They have me cold. I knew what I was getting into. Now it's time to pay the tollbooth man. So I'll tell you what I need from you."

"Anything, friend."

"The peeping tom novel is done, and I have two others ready to go. My publishers—hell, no one is going to want to print my books with the record I'll have. Who wants the scandal? The boys in Manhattan only like scandals from afar, scandals they can sell but not be touched by. What I want you to do is go into my trailer, before the cops get themselves a warrant—and maybe they have already—and rescue my three novel manuscripts. They're about 210 pages each, standard length. I sure as hell don't want the D.A. to use the peeper book as evidence against me. Like you said, the research defense ain't a-gonna fly. Grab any other incriminating manuscripts you might find, I forget what I have—partials to unfinished books, short stories, ideas for books, whatever. Grab them and run. Wait awhile, and then send them out with your name on them. Publish the stuff. Some may say you're imitating me, but what the hell, I imitate James M. Cain and Jim Thompson."

I couldn't believe what I was hearing.

"I'm not going to put my name on your work!" I said.

"My name is mud, boy, and I don't want that work to go for naught. You're due for a novel, but you won't sit down and do the work, so take my work and have your novel—three novels."

"It's not right."

"Right and wrong has nothing to do with it."

"Your publishers...."

"The hell with those crooks," Roger said. "If you don't want to put your name on them, then put another name, come up with a good *nom de plume*, I just want to see, by next year, as I am doing my five years or less, the damn things out in the world."

I gave in.

I agreed.

It was time for me to go.

The cops there were wondering what I wanted with the peeper, and I just shrugged and said, "You can never tell about people in the world."

I was still the hero.

"Like Fremont's floozy wife," one cop said.

"Great body on that dame," another said.

"The broad is a bad egg," a third said.

The second one laughed and said, "And she probably thought when she bumped the old bastard, she was going to get all his money and property."

They all laughed.

"What's funny?" I asked.

The first cop said, "Old man Fremont changed his will three days ago. Everything he owned goes to the local hospital to build a new children's wing. Hot little Mrs. Fremont doesn't get a shiny dime."

* * * * * * *

That night—although I would not hear about it until later—Eve hanged herself in her cell, using her garter and nylons.

10.

I couldn't tell if the cops had been through Roger's trailer or not, it was such an unorganized mess, accompanied by the usual smells of stale and unwashed things, dust and grime, and the atmosphere of the lonely.

I should have come by more often and talked to him, I thought. I should have convinced him not to get too deep into the head of his fictional character, so much that he became that person.

Oh, there were many "I should haves" going through my mind. I should have helped Kay with her drinking; I should have never gotten involved with a young girl and I should have been more careful in bed; I should have never succumbed to Eve and her body and her promises of money and a better life.

I should have never been born.

I found Roger's three manuscripts. They were titled *The Sin Pepper*, *Lust Lure*, and *Tramp Wife in Yellow Halter and White Shorts*.

I found some unpublished stories and ideas for books jotted down on half sheets of paper and napkins.

I gathered all the originals and carbons and took them with me.

I also took the four beers and the bottle of rye that were in the fridge.

I took them and ran.

I ran far away.

I told myself I wouldn't look back.

* * * * * *

But I did look back. I looked in the papers for news about Roger, who was pleading guilty and getting three years in prison. He'd probably only do a year and a half, maybe two, on good behavior, but knowing Roger Weaver, he would not maintain any sort of good behavior locked up—not without booze and cigarettes and a typewriter. I imagined him standing in the middle of the prison yard, telling wild entertaining stories of men who were heels and women who were wayward wantons, in exchange for cigarettes and fermented rotting fruit.

Roger Weaver: incarcerated Homer.

As for his books, I did sent them to the paperback publishers, using an agent in New York as a go-between, under the name K. Adams. All three were picked up by one of Roger's usual publishers—Comfy Books—at $700 each. "The new Roger Weaver!" one editor wrote.

I sent Roger a note: *Three homeruns.*

He wrote back: *!!!*

I even started a novel based on one of Roger's ideas, but I could only get as far as page eleven.

* * * * * * *

I lived in a rooming house for three months, quietly working as a farmhand nearby. By day, I worked bales of hay and helped bulls mate with the cows; by night, I sat down at my typewriter in my small room, and worked on some stories and other things.

I couldn't finish a damn thing.

K. Adams may have been the bright new pulp writer on the scene, but Jack Card was washed up.

My life was unfinished.

There was something I had to do.

I couldn't stop thinking about her.

And our child.

I had to find Lucy.

* * * * * * *

It took me two weeks, but it wasn't that hard to find her. I knew where she had grown up in Pennsylvania. It was just a matter of finding what hills and what shack, and when I did, I

VIOLENCE IS THE ONLY SOLUTION

3 VIC POWERS CRIME TALES

GARY LOVISI

THE BORGO PRESS

MMXII

VIOLENCE IS THE ONLY SOLUTION

Copyright © 1993, 1995, 1999, 2012 by Gary Lovisi

FIRST EDITION

Published by Wildside Press LLC

www.wildsidebooks.com

DEDICATION

For Lucille, as always

CONTENTS

ACKNOWLEDGMENTS

"Violence Is the Only Solution" was first published in *Blood in Brooklyn*, Do Not Pr, 1995. Copyright © 1995, 2012 by Gary Lovisi.

"Dogs Know" was first published in *100 Dastardly Little Detective Stories*, edited by Robert Weinberg, Stefan Dziemianowicz, and Martin H. Greenberg, Barnes & Noble, 1993. Copyright © 1993, 2012 by Gary Lovisi.

"Black Vomit" was first published in *Dirty Dogs: A Wolf-Pack Collection of Vic Powers Crime Stories*, Gryphon Books, 1999. Copyright © 1999, 2012 by Gary Lovisi.

VIOLENCE IS
THE ONLY SOLUTION

I believe in homicide.

I've always believed.

It's just the way things turned out for me. There was no choice. No alternative I could ever see. The choice was simple, kill the evil or let it devour you. And let me tell you, the evil has one hell of an appetite. Ever since I was a kid. It was always so damn hungry.

I've lived a while, done some things, been involved in some things. Killing has never really bothered me. Not all that much. As long as it was some scumbag who deserved killing that is, and Lord knows there's plenty of those.

I am always careful though. Usually. It's crucial. So I always make sure. Never break my Golden Rule. Never, ever kill an innocent person. Never! That's the one sure way to damnation. And that's a road down into Hell you do not want to take.

My one law is this: if you're not sure a person is an "innocent," then don't do it. Just don't do it. Do not do it. Leave them alone. Walk away. If you gotta, run away.

But that's all by and by what was on my mind lately.

I was beginning to get a might testy with my country recently. Stuff I'd found out about the Vietnam MIAs, two different CIAs fighting a secret war with each other and the dirty deals to open trade with the same people in 'Nam who had murdered our soldiers. Others doing worse, selling children for sex in Thailand. To American buyers. Sex tourists. I'd like to crack their heads. The sellers and the buyers. Keep that whole market underground where it belongs, six feet underground.

I thought of crazy Jack Rodríguez, blasting away at Congress, a man who had originally been imprisoned unjustly, then who had unwittingly discovered a secret book that I had mailed to the *Washington Post*. A book that had disappeared like it had never existed at all. I mean, Amelia Earhart and Jimmy Hoffa had nothing on disappearances when it came to that damn book being lost and forgotten. And the information in that book? Well, I knew now it would never, ever, see the light of day.

Then there was Rodney King, the L.A. Riots, Ruby Ridge, Waco, the O.J. fiasco, Oklahoma City, all war cries in certain circles. Then there was a slew of recent court verdicts in trials that split the country right down the middle, splitting Americans against each other, not to mention a presidential campaign and fund-raising scam that was so crooked it made Tricky Dick Nixon look like a novice and a downright "honorable" SOB by comparison! It was so bad it might even bring down another American president!

Of course, it was all common sense to see and to figure out, but common sense solutions didn't seem to matter much in America any more. Talk about the damn Snail Darter? Common sense was the real "endangered species" in the 1990s in America.

My country had become a nation where one side was forever at war against the other, and everyone had to choose up sides to survive, and there was no one left honest enough to say the truth. Or powerful enough to say the truth and get away with it. Without getting screwed. So he or she wouldn't have their life and career destroyed. We were fast becoming a nation of sheep, where racists of every type, politically-correct storm troopers, self-serving hypocrites, and lying demagogues bought their way to power and out of crimes any average Joe or Jane would see serious prison time for. And no one seemed to care or know what to do about it.

I'd had it with all the bullshit!

It seemed that everyone from mutant Klan and Nazi morons

to anti-White racist Black militants and irate hate-filled Muslin sects was in our face every day lately. Shouting, "Kill the evil White Man!"

"Kill the damn Blacks!"

"Kill the Jews!"

"Kill the...."

Well, you can fill in the blank.

"Kill them all!" is all too many people only understand. Everyone at each other's throats. All the problems, all the pain, all the lies—because all the time the implication too often seemed that violence was the only solution to the problems we faced.

As a nation. As individuals.

It's in the news every single day.

It made me so sick.

You see, I understand violence.

That's why it sickens me.

Yeah, me, Vic Powers, killer and louse, and a real bad guy. Some say too dangerous to let live. Them that tried to alter that reality are no longer with us. Yeah, so I'm a bad one. Sometimes. But I'm not an evil one.

And there's a big difference.

I admit it. I've committed homicide. I believe in homicide. Sometimes it's the only way to fight the true Evil. Or to fix something that's gotten way out of hand and needs to be fixed real bad.

You see, I know Evil too. Evil never gives up. It never goes away. Evil is hungry. Always hungry. Insatiable.

It never stops.

See, I don't believe that Good can ever triumph over Evil like a lot of the fools do. I've seen too much not to know how things really work. Evil is just too strong, too incredibly relentless. In any kind of fair fight between Good and Evil, Evil will always win. Evil is tougher, stronger, Evil knows all the dirty tricks and uses them to devastating effect. Good is not single-minded or persistent. When Good guys win they pack it in and go home.

The war's over for them. Good guys don't understand that while a battle may end, the war never ends. The war is never over. Evil never quits.

Now let's say you put up Bad against Evil. Now, that's a different story. That's where I come in. Bad will use Evil's ways against itself. Like I do. Like I use homicide.

I'm not afraid of taking care of a scumbag who deserves it either. I believe in homicide. So I'll kill, but only those that deserve it—and there's a lot deserving, believe me. But I'll never cross over. Never kill an innocent. Never.

* * * * * * *

I wondered who I was kidding. I'm telling myself this stuff and it ain't exactly true. I crossed over. Once. Killed an innocent person. It was horrible. I'm not proud to say it. It damn near destroyed me and it's something I'll have remorse over and be ashamed of until the day I die. And I deserved every bit of pain I got from it and every bit of pain I gave myself from it too. I ain't complaining, but it happened. I'll never do it again. I'll never cross over again. I'll be real careful.

But I still believe in homicide.

That's the way I am.

And even with all this stuff in my head, all this pain and rage and fire eating away at me, I still wanted to have a life. Like, a normal life. Sorta. Like what could pass as normal for me, Vic Powers. Something like my old partner Larry had made for himself so many years ago when we'd been on the job together. It seemed like another life now. Looking back. So far away. So long ago. But I had wanted that once. That road Larry had marked out to me back then—he'd made it all seem so clear and attainable, living a wholesome life, having a good loving woman at your side, raising children, loving them. Building a home together. Something for the future. Larry had shown me the way. And I wanted to follow his lead, his excellent example. At least, I'd wanted to follow it as best I could. At least I wanted to try.

But it was not for me.

And besides, it didn't seem like the country would let me, things just kept getting in my way.

It was weird. I'd just walked into this situation, and now it was left up to me—Vic Powers, of all people—to uphold the middle ground of tolerance and sanity against violent extremes full of lunatics who were dangerous hateful killers. I'd fallen into a world headed for the dumpster at supersonic speed and even though I held all the pieces—naturally at the time—I had no idea of any of what was really going on.

All I knew was that things had been going down in America the last few years, a lot of stuff really scared me. Some things I had been involved in. Some things I had seen. Some I had heard about. It got me nervous. Now it seemed I was the one who might have to set some things right.

And that was the scariest thought of all to me.

Had we sunk that low?

* * * * * * *

It started out as a missing person case. Evolved into a runaway. Then went to hell from there on. There was this couple and they had a daughter. She was twenty-something years old. Blonde, cute, and probably hot and horny. Looking for thrills or action or something. Maybe just to get away? To run? Freedom? Safety? I'd find out.

I was called over to the Rauch apartment. Swanky place on West Street. They gave me photos of their daughter.

I said, "I'll need info about all her friends, her hang-out places, stuff like that, so I can find her."

The father told me, "You don't need that."

The mother said, "It's not that Lori is missing, Mr. Powers. Not exactly. You see, we know where she is. That's the problem."

"You'll have to explain that to me. On the phone you said it was a simple missing person case."

"It is, Mr. Powers. Lori is missing, but it's simple because we know where she is."

I said, "Okay. Maybe we should try again? What exactly is the problem if you know where Lori is?"

"That is the problem, Mr. Powers. It's because of where she is. That's what bothers Morris and me so much," Mrs. Rauch said. She looked over to her husband nervously, he sighed, got up and walked away. He looked sad, beaten down, a defeated man. There were tears in the wife's eyes as she watched him.

As he walked off he said, "I wish I could kill them. I wish I could kill them all with my bare hands but violence is never a solution to our problems, Mr. Powers. I believe that. I have to."

I laughed, said, "Violence is never a solution to our problems? Just look around you, every damn minute of every damn day in this stinking world violence is being used to solve problems."

There was silence while Morris looked at me and then left the room.

His wife sat across from me, sighed deeply, said, "It's just so hard to talk about it."

"I know," I lied. I had no idea.

"You know, I married Morris after Bill, my husband, died. That was almost four years ago."

I didn't say anything, I just watched the wife wring her hands like they were an old mop, shaking them and then her head, like it was all so terrible, trying to summon up the courage to tell me something unbelievable.

I said softly, "Go on, Mrs. Rauch, it's best to tell it, get it all out."

She sighed, said, "Morris is Jewish."

I smiled, "I sorta figured that."

She nodded. "You don't know what it's been like for us, Mr. Powers. My family is old Catholic and I was raised strict Catholic. Morris is Jewish and a very good man, but not a particularly religious one. He'd lost family in the Holocaust. So while he is naturally cynical toward God and religion, he does have a very strong Jewish identity. Culturally. Do you know what I mean?"

I nodded. I think I knew what she meant.

"Anyway," she continued, "Morris and I have known each other for a long time, a very long time. Long ago, when we were young, we were...but we could never, never think of marriage in those days. Things were so different then. There was the family situation. My father. Morris's mother. It was so impossible. You understand?"

I nodded. A lot of stuff was different in the old days, twenty-to-thirty years ago, maybe even five-to-ten years ago in some places, with some people. Lotta changes. Some for the better, some for the worse. Stupid bigotry that kept lovers apart was some of that Evil.

I figured it was just the Shit Quotient making itself known again. Somehow it always stayed the same in the world—things change, times change, sometimes a real lot of changes—but the Shit Quotient always remains at the same level. The Shit Quotient is the one constant in an ever-changing world. Some people are treated like hell, screwed over, killed, but somewhere else others have it all sweet and easy. Then the world tilts and things change. The Shit Quotient kicks in and those people get beat up, robbed, raped, hurt, killed. It's always the same. It's just that it is not always the same people. Or the same type of people. Or people from the same country. Jews, Armenians, American Indians, Colonial settlers, Slavs, Mayans, white Dominicans, Haitians under the Ton-ton, Khmer Rouge piling up the bones of fellow Cambodians, Iraqi poison gas...it never ends.

I figured the Shit Quotient was kicking in again in America.

I sighed, looked over at Mrs. Rauch, and I just knew she was about to tell me some sad sack crap that I did not want to hear, that I did not want to know about, and that I was sure would make me angry and sick and probably want to do something seriously bad to stop it.

I also knew that she didn't feel right talking about it. She had pride. She was ashamed.

I said, "It's all right, get it out. Tell me the whole story, Mrs. Rauch."

She sighed, "It's so terrible, Mr. Powers, so...so...."

She didn't know how to describe it. I knew.

"Evil?" I offered.

She looked into my eyes then for the first time, staring, and I knew, and she knew.

She finally said, "Yes. That's the word for it, Mr. Powers. Evil."

I felt the nape hairs on my neck tingle, then nodded, waiting for her to begin.

"I wasn't watching, you always have to watch, Mr. Powers. If you don't watch, it.... Evil, will spring up on you. I know now, it's always there. Waiting. I'm sure of it. Now. It happened like that with Morris and me, we didn't realize about Lori, how serious things had become, until it was too late. My God!"

"Realize what, Mrs. Rauch?"

She was flustered, beginning to cry. I watched the tears stream down her face. I didn't try to comfort her. Her sobs grew louder and terrible to hear. It was like she'd lost her daughter, like she'd lost her to death, killed, murdered, but of course it wasn't anything like that at all. Lori wasn't physically dead at all, as far as I could tell. No, that wasn't it. It was far worse. It was a deeper and darker loss. Lori was not dead, but she was just as dead as if she were dead, and in some ways she was deader than any of the dead. The one thing in Mrs. Rauch's life she had loved had turned out rotten, and now the Evil had Lori within its grasp and was beginning to squeeze.

I knew Morris would come back eventually. He looked a mess now. I could see the pain in his face, the sorrow in his eyes. I'd seen cheerier faces in old photos of Nazi concentration camp victims. It was scary. It haunted me. His gaze was deep, his eyes like tombstones, with ovens in them, and skeletons crying out in pain and rage. Forever. I had to shake my head to clear my mind.

I looked away from Morris and his pain, I knew all about

that stuff. There was something else there in his eyes that made me want to look though. It was the man's deep love for his wife and his longing to ease her own pain. It made him come out of himself, to step outside of his own terrible distress, to comfort his wife, to hold her, to tell her how much he loved her.

I didn't say anything. I didn't have to. I got the picture all right—when Morris handed me the photo.

The photo that showed Lori, all pale and blonde and blue-eyed, young and shiny, with that lovely smile of hers. She was a pretty girl. Pretty special.

She was dressed in a white shirt, starched insignia on the collars, right armband boldly proclaiming something that disgusted all sane people, a silver death's head in the center of her black field cap, smiling. Anticipating. Hungry. Her black boots shined to a glow, the gun in her hand cocked and apparently ready to be fired, the man next to her holding a large framed photograph of Adolf Hitler in one hand, and a Nazi swastika flag in the other. Lori and the man with her in the photo were smiling. Likely thinking some pure Aryan-type thoughts.

Morris Rauch handed me the photograph.

I took it, put it away in my pocket.

"This filth.... I...I...oh, my God! Why, after all these years, and all we have been through?"

"I'll find her and I'll bring her back."

Morris Rauch looked up at me then, "I don't even know if I want her back, Mr. Powers."

I said, "Look, she's fallen in with evil people, but...."—and I was gonna give the, 'but she's still your daughter', spiel. But, of course, she wasn't—his daughter—that is.

"Bad companions, Mr. Powers? Is that what you think this is? This is a bit deeper than that. These are Nazis, Mr. Powers, not some group of rambunctious kids."

I nodded. But I knew things weren't always that simple, either. There had to be more to this than met the eye. As it would turn out, there was.

* * * * * * *

It's a funny thing about being twisted. The right amount of pressure and the wrong ideas can sure bring out amazing things in some people. I remember years ago when the KKK had been very active against Jews in Alabama, the Feds eventually found that the guy responsible for all the pain and problems down there against the Jews, the local KKK Grand Dragon, had actually been born a Jew.

Then there was Wayne Williams, a successful, young black man from Atlanta, and a serial murderer of twenty-nine of Atlanta's black children. He figured that he could improve the black race by killing off all the poor and uneducated black children. There's a man could've won a lifetime membership in the KKK.

Twisted.

I didn't even want to think about where Vic Powers fit in all that but I could sure understand it. Anger and hatred is a deadly mix. I feel the anger. But, none of the hate—except hate for haters. I do hate the haters.

And I sure do understand anger.

* * * * * * *

When I got back to my car I sat there a while and studied the photo. It was from a few years ago. Thing was, if Lori Rauch had run off to join the local Fourth Reich Nazi and Klan gang, it might take a bit of work to get her out of there. Especially since she was, apparently, a part of the problem now. I knew something else too, the guy in the photo with Lori, was Arthur Burk. He was trouble. He had been a young Aryan skinhead who'd since gone legit (sort of) and was sporting a more rational political line. Hey, Communists use the cover of the left and liberals all the time, so why not the other way around? David Duke was just one former American Nazi who came to my mind. Farrakhan is another Nazi, only he comes in a different color.

Burk didn't wear Nazi uniforms any longer. He'd gone legit long ago, like David Duke, but he was the same swine he always was. Aiming now to be a legit pol. I'd heard of him. He was dangerous. He had four things that made him dangerous. He was serious, he was smart, he had a lot of money backing him from somewhere, and he had heavy connections. Favors owed. He was also a good-looking ladies man and could be a very charming fellow when it suited his purpose. He also was something else. He was not as racist as he let on that he was. He was just an opportunist who was into death and destruction for its own sake. And to use people. And death. And now, apparently, Lori. All for his own ends.

He was also a man with a plan.

* * * * * * *

I asked around, from the local riff-raff and some people I knew in some pretty unsavory organizations, radical offshoots of the old Jewish Defense League, some right-wing loonies, lefty leftovers of the old Communist Workers Party. I found out some amazing things. I was surprised by it all.

There seemed to be a lot of stuff going on in the hate underground lately. Things were a hop, skip, and a jump more extreme than the merely radical underground that most people are aware of. The talkers.

The hate underground is something else. The hate underground was making ready for war. The problem with them is that they're not just 'talkers', a lot of them are 'doers'. Timothy McVeigh? Silent, but a doer. You get my drift? From what I found out something big was in the works and they were just waiting for the word.

I didn't really want to get involved in all that crap now. All I wanted to do was find Lori and bring her home. Maybe slap some sense into her on the ride back? Maybe not. I didn't know what I could do or say to make her come back. Not home, but to reality. Show her photos of death camp survivors? Play on her empathy? If she had any? If she really was in with these people she'd spout the line, it was all made up, some Jewish conspiracy, and she'd just laugh it all off. And that would drive me nuts and then I'd knock her block off. Her mind and soul may have fallen so deeply into the dark pit of hatred that I could never really save her. It's damn deep and dark in there. Like a black hole. No light escapes once its fallen within. Neither does anything else. Maybe even Lori.

The Fourth Reich Klan skinheads had places all over the country. Safe houses and club houses and such. Rat trap bars and hole-in-the-wall skell joints. Most of the members and hangers-on didn't amount to much, a bunch of two-bit loser-haters, the kind of kid, and later on adult, who always blames someone else for their own miserable problems. Never realizing that we make our own hell. But once in a while the group would latch on to a real hardcore bad guy with balls. One that was either too stupid or too full of hate to back down. A doer. An action-oriented type of guy.

The kind they'd send up the line, up through the network, one who could be useful for bigger things. It was a kind of upward mobility program for hate mongers.

It was like that in the Fourth Reich Klan skinheads.

It was also like that in the elite Fruit of Mecca killers, among the leadership of the Bloods (who were national now), the old Chinese gang Born to Kill (BTK) making a comeback, the Black Liberation Army still full of hate and out to kill white cops, the Chicago El Ricans who had worked for the government of Libya, the Yahwahs whose "charming" organization originated as a prison rape gang, the old hardcore KKK that wanted revenge, the enforcement arm of the Latin Kings who wanted respect, the old Ghost Shadows now in the Tongs of every Chinatown across the nation and in the heroin trade big-time, the Crips who worked with Hell's Angels, the radical Jewish Kahane-hai loaded and ready to fight, Aryan Nations and the Eoleim City leaders wanting to spill blood, the old Mafia and the new drug Mafia out to take their turf back, the

Russian Mafia, vicious and violent Columbian and Nigerian gangs and wicked Jamaican posses, and all the various Arab and anti-American terrorist cells that were sitting and planning and waiting patiently. There were Chinese Triads, and Japanese *Yakuza* here in cities doing their work, international drug cartel guys, rich arms merchants always ready to bring in a shipment for a good cause, South African racists with no place left to go, right-wing anti-abortion nuts and left-wing neo-hippy environmental unibomber type thugs, and animal rights crazies who'd kill you for wearing leather shoes or a wool scarf in the winter. And a lot more who were even crazier like the Nambla and pedophile gangs.

It was always the same shit. Since Garfield, since McKinley, since Kennedy and Oswald and King with James Earl Ray. Find the real crazies and then use them to deal out more pain, deal out more death and destruction, all for the 'glorious cause' or to 'save' America.

Bullshit!

All that ever happens is that a lot of innocent people, usually women and children, end up getting hurt or killed. People that aren't involved in any of this crap in any way and have no idea what the hell is really going on. Like in Oklahoma City, they're the ones that are always hurt or killed. Average citizens just trying to live their lives, earn a living, feed their kids, put a roof over their heads, blown up or murdered. Or politicians, killed for what? Words? Ideas? Talk? I know, I don't like politicians, or lawyers either, but that's a different matter. All I knew was that Lori was damn deep into this kind of shit. It all made me so damn sick. So damn angry.

* * * * * * *

From what I'd been able to find out, Arthur Burk's organization owned some country club in the New Jersey boondocks where Lori was supposed to be working. I found out that her job was head of security for the Fourth Reich Klan skinheads.

That kinda blew me the wrong way to hear that. That's a leadership role. That means serious ideological commitment. I knew it sure as hell would make a hard job that much tougher. And it could get me killed a lot easier and quicker than I thought might be possible.

There was supposed to be some kind of big meeting at this country club in a few days. Lori was supposedly there early with a few of her goons to check out the place and prepare it. I figured I'd sneak in, grab her, then be out before I got caught. Or killed. At least, I hoped so. I'd gotten into better protected places, after all. I thought of Casarella, Loring, others.

So I drove on out to the Jersey boonies Tuesday night. Decided I'd sneak onto the grounds after midnight, then lay low until I could find Lori when she came back Wednesday morning. Getting into the grounds was no problem. I caught a big break because the dogs were all kenneled out by the barn. It was dark and quiet. A guard was here and there but nothing serious right now, it was still too early for the big Friday night meeting. That would be when security really got serious.

* * * * * * *

I eventually made it to the clubhouse without being spotted. It was a huge building with a large central meeting area. I didn't see anyone. I headed down into the basement to hide out until dawn. Later I'd scout the area and try to get to Lori. At least that was the master plan. Not one of my better plans to be sure. Especially once I discovered that I was hiding out in the middle of a basement full of high explosives. The whole damn place was loaded with crates of weapons, as well as C-4, dynamite, and other ordnance, even grenades and bombs. It looked like the place was stuffed to the rafters with every damn kind of weapon and device invented by man to kill as many other men as possible. Being down there with all those explosives made me glad that I had quit smoking years ago, but I could've sure used a good stiff drink just then.

* * * * * * *

Wednesday came and went and no Lori. I tried to be cool, stay hidden. Things were still quiet outside but once in a while one of the Nazi goons would come downstairs and get a weapon or a box of shells. Then I'd hide and hope he wouldn't find me. They didn't, so far.

Once I heard two guys at the foot of the stairs talking about the big meeting.

"We'll bring the fuckin' country right to its knees!" one of them said.

"And set it right again! The way we want it to be."

The other replied, "Freakin' right, Brother! To its knees! Bleeding all the way down. Burk will rip America a brand new asshole!"

They laughed then and went away. It didn't sound encouraging. Something big was up. But what? I let it pass for the moment.

I just couldn't figure it. I couldn't see how a bunch of freaks and geek Nazi morons could ever bring America to its knees. First off, there weren't nowheres enough of them. And they weren't really organized, they didn't take orders or have direction, they were lazy misfits and losers. Except for a very few like Arthur Burk, they really were just a bunch of overweight hateful losers. But then I thought about how the original Nazi movement had begun so long ago in Germany. I thought about Hitler and his Brownshirts, and they were thought to be a bunch of crude, beer-hall assholes, and they'd damn near destroyed the world once. Not to mention killing tens of millions of people. And now I wasn't so sure about anything anymore. I began to feel a chill down there sitting alone in that Nazi cache basement full of explosives. And it didn't have anything to do with the cool seventy-degree summer temperature outside. It was a chill about the future, about my country.

* * * * * * *

So Wednesday came and went. Uneventful. By Thursday morning it was a different story. Now things were really hopping. I heard big trucks and a lot of voices, frenzied activity in the hall above me and all around the grounds. The dogs were let loose now, being led around the grounds by armed handlers wearing your traditional Nazi Brownshirt uniform complete with Swastika armbands. Kinda made me feel like I'd fallen into some bizarre World War II movie. But this was no damn movie, this was the stinking end of 1997 and there was no big John Wayne or Audie Murphy out there to save my miserable ass if I fucked up on this one.

All the time I hid out I was looking for Lori, but the words of those two goons from the day before went around and around in my head. I decided that I might need some insurance, some serious insurance, so I set to work, found some wires, a miniature electronic detonator, rigged the whole damn mess and then slipped the small duct-tape wrapped package into the pocket of my green jacket. It was too hot to wear the damn thing in the summer heat, so I carried it as I left the basement, as I moved up into the big hall above.

*　*　*　*　*　*　*

It was Thursday night and it was dark and quiet, but I didn't let that fool me. There were enemies all over the place. All around me. No, I wasn't paranoid. I was being commonsensical. Imagine that, me, Vic Powers, and common sense. I smiled. The world can sometimes become so very weird.

I saw that the main floor of the huge hall was loaded with people talking and shouting and cursing and threats filled the air. It sounded hot. Explosive. It was so loud in the room but it was all muffled and fuzzy outside, where I was, in the outer hall. The huge dark wood doors were closed shut, tighter than a crack whore's heart. In front of those doors, amazingly, instead of finding armed guards, I saw a tripod display stand with a large sign on it that said: "Welcome: Sales Reps—to the

National Conference!"

I didn't know what the hell to make of that. It sure didn't seem like Nazis to put on a sales conference, but I let it pass for the moment. It was strange though, and I began to wonder if I'd done some Rip Van Winkle scene when suddenly the outside door opened wide and I saw Lori Rauch enter with a squad of storm trooper goons following behind her.

I froze for a moment. Stunned. She looked my way. I gave her a Nazi salute, then opened the two big doors and entered the assembly room as fast as I could. My heart was in my mouth and my nerves were frazzled to the limit as I waited for Lori and her goon squad to come in after me and pound my head into the floor. But they didn't. They didn't have to. I'd walked right into a huge chamber full of every kind of Nazi, skinhead, neo-Nazi and race-conscious Aryan thug and Klan monster in the country. They seemed to all be there, having some kind of big secret meeting, dozens of them were seated around this huge circular table. I shuddered. There were so many of them. Just my dumb luck, it looked like they'd moved up their meeting by one day and I'd fallen right into it.

Then I heard the voice, and my name.

"Well, well, if it isn't Vic Powers."

It was a male voice, rough, hard, deadly.

I grimaced. I looked to where the voice was coming from and saw Arthur Burk, older now, and meaner, stand up and come toward me. Along with him came a dozen of the biggest and nastiest looking white guys I'd ever seen this side of the WWF. They were all armed. I was wishing that I was also, though in that company it would not have done me the least bit of good

Burk was older, I remembered him now, and he had filled out from the way he'd looked years ago when he'd been a lanky skinhead and half-assed crim. Larry and I had busted him a decade or more back when I'd been on the cops. Burk had been penny-ante back then, but he did have brains and balls. He went away and came back meaner and worse than ever. Prison, the 'University of Crime,' had never turned out a more hardcore nor devoted graduate.

I could see it in his face. Now it was his revenge time.

"You remember me, I see," Burk told me, smiling wickedly as his cold eyes bore down into my own blank orbs.

It must have been like looking in a mirror for him, and he soon turned away. His goons grabbed me, frisked me, then held me. Hard and fast. I didn't see any sense in starting a fight just then with over a dozen Nazi killers so I opted for conversation with the Führer junior instead.

"Yeah," I said. "I remember you, and you remember me."

"You sent me away."

I said, "It wasn't long enough, apparently."

He laughed. Saw me look around, said, "Oh, you mean all this? This is nothing. Nothing. Tomorrow, Mr. Powers, that is the day that will go down in history."

He saw that I didn't know what he was talking about. He liked that. It made him feel like a big man. Powerful. Important. I guess he was, for the moment. Until I got to him, that is. But I put that on hold, too, now. I didn't particularly care about all this stuff, my mind was working overtime figuring on just what the hell I was going to do to get my ass out of this mess. I was not encouraged by the way things seemed to be going at the moment.

Burk continued, "I know all about you coming here, trying to rescue my Lori, so you can bring her back to that old Jew stepfather and her whore mother—that bitch of a race traitor."

"Now you sound like a real Nazi."

He slapped my face, back and forth.

"Listen to me!" he barked.

"I'm listening!" I shouted back at him.

He smiled, "That's better. Of course you realize that when you go to the underground for information your very inquiry becomes information that can also be sold on the same market. Your asking about Lori? Me? Our little group? The very people you are asking let us know who has been doing the asking. And why. It's basic shit, Powers."

I nodded. "I know how things work, but it got me here to Lori. To you. Didn't it?"

"And you'll die for it. Like all race traitors will."

I got a bit offended, said, "So now you're calling me a race traitor?"

"Whites who go against white supremacy. Whites who are traitors to their race, who oppose our goals, are traitors to their race. Just like you, Powers."

I laughed at that. "I'm no race traitor."

"You're white, aren't you?" Burk sneered.

"I'm white, but that's just skin color. My race, asshole, my fucking RACE—is not WHITE—it's HUMAN! That's what binds us all together. That's the only 'racism' I believe in. It's you and your kind, in whatever color you come in, that are the true race traitors—traitors to the one race we are all a part of. The only race that's important. The HUMAN race."

Burk laughed. "Nice speech, Powers."

"I thought you might like it."

He smacked me in the face. "I don't, but that doesn't matter. After tomorrow this will all be sorted out. There'll be a new America. One where 'blood in the face' will rule, where all whites will stand together against the 'mud people'."

"I don't think so, asshole," I said.

"A lot of Americans are listening to us now."

"Yeah, and a lot of people would tell you how good shit tastes if it came in a different flavor. But it's still just shit!" I barked.

Arthur Burk smiled. It got me nervous. He wasn't angry, he was confident. He said, "Take him out and kill him!"

The goons dragged me off, as I heard guns cocked, rounds loaded into chambers, bolts pulled back. The army was getting ready for action. On me.

Then....

"Wait!" Burk suddenly ordered. He came over to me, looking me up and down carefully. "You really don't understand what this is all about, do you? Well, I'm going to give you a wonderful opportunity, Powers. I'm going to keep you alive just a bit longer so you can see what I am talking about. I want you to see my plan for America's future."

I didn't say a word.

Burk added, with laughter, "You know, Powers, you're a fool. Always were. You should join us. I'm white, you're white. We're all white here. And I know you don't like niggers. Ain't I right, Powers?"

I didn't say anything.

He insisted that I answer. He slapped my face back and forth, asking the question again and again.

"You don't like niggers! I know it, Powers!"

I glared at him, finally I growled, "I don't like niggers, but I like Black people! There is a difference and I know the difference! And I don't like White niggers either, asshole!"

Burk grew red.

I waited for what I figured was on the way.

Then he just laughed, said, "That doesn't matter any more, Powers. Nothing matters any more after tomorrow. You see, my problems aren't with the niggers or even the queers or the damn Jews and the ZOG, my problems are more focused. My problems are with the whites that have sold out their race, their children, and their blood. They're the ones I'm after. They're all cowards, and they'll bend if I put enough pressure on them—like if I kill a few—which I am all set to do. They either climb on board with me and my program—or they'll drown in the mud. And, Powers, eventually, and you know it—they'll come to me! Eventually. There will be no alternative after tomorrow."

I didn't know what the hell to say. So I said nothing.

I sweated bullets as they dragged me away.

They chained me to a wall in a back room of one of the numerous outbuildings on the country club grounds. I think it was a storage room of the damn pro shop.

Lori Rauch came to see me about an hour later. She was dressed in her best Nazi-bitch uniform and shiny black boots. She left her goons outside, but she still held a gun on me. It didn't matter at that point because there wasn't much I could do about anything.

"So you are the man my mother hired?"

"Your mother and father love you very much. They want you to come home."

"Liar! And don't ever say that that old Jew is my father. He is my step-father. He is a Jew and I hate him!"

Well, I saw where this was going. I just laughed at her. It really was quite funny to my warped sense of humor.

My laughing shocked her, surprised her, not at all what she expected.

"Don't laugh!"

Which just made me laugh at her all the more.

"Why are you laughing at me?" she asked. Then demanded.

I couldn't help it. I said: "I was just thinking about twisted people."

She slapped me. Hard.

I just laughed harder, almost hysterical now.

I saw her finger twitch on the trigger of the gun in her hand. She slapped me again.

I just couldn't stop laughing.

"Stop laughing at me!" she screamed.

Then she kicked me in the gut. I doubled over. It hurt, she had good aim, but I just kept on laughing. I don't think I could have stopped even had I wanted to just then.

"Fucking son-of-a-bitch! I'll kill you!" and she lowered her weapon at me and meant it.

Between laughing I was able to utter, "Well, then you'll never know why I'm laughing at you, will you, Lori?"

And that just made me laugh all the harder.

She stopped, and lowered her weapon away from me.

I don't know how it happened, but I just stopped laughing then.

She looked at me like I was a mad man.

Which I'm sure that at that moment, I was.

I took a deep breath, said, "It really is funny. I mean, if you have any sense of humor, Lori, especially a macabre sense of humor like I do, you'll just love this. I'm sure even you will find it hysterically funny."

"What!" she shouted.

"About you. About Morris Rauch. I hate to break it to you, Lori, but Morris isn't your step-father—he's your real father."

She was stunned for a second, her face grew red with rage and then she shouted, "Liar! Bloody liar!"

I shrugged and laughed.

Then I got another slap in the face, this time with the pistol barrel. It was her best hit on me yet.

"Pig!" she cried.

"It's true," I said, with a smaller laugh this time, I didn't want any of my loose teeth to fall out as I talked.

That last slap had also opened up my cheek. "And the best part of it all," I laughed, "is that that makes you Jewish! Which I think is a hell of a funny irony, just as long as your Nazi friends don't find out."

"Fucking liar!" she screamed.

I smiled, "It's no lie, Lori." Now I had to talk fast and I knew it. "I have proof. Your mother and Morris were lovers many years back. They were lovers but could never marry because religious and ethnic barriers were just too impossible to overcome back then with their families. But, Lori, they were in love and they still are, and your mother had a daughter by Morris, and it was you. And then, when Morris went off to fight in Vietnam, your mother met Bill—the man you believe is your father. But Morris is your real father. And I have proof...."

But I didn't get to say any more because I got a steel-shod boot in the face that knocked me down and she stormed out so fast it was all like a blur from a tornado.

* * * * * * *

Time passed. I tried to mend my wounds and pride as best I could. Took a hell of a beating from that girl, worse than what Burk had done to me. Those damn rings on Lori's fingers had done a nasty job on my face and head, not to mention that gun barrel upside my skull. To say nothing of her Nazi jackboots slamming into my gut and groin. But all that was the least of my problems. I had to figure a way to get out of here and I didn't see any way I could break these chains. And I didn't want to think about what that meant for my future prospects, severely limited as they apparently were.

I dozed off, and was in my thirteenth nightmare when the door to the storage room groaned open and Lori came back inside. Quietly. She was alone.

She wasn't dressed in Nazi crap this time. She didn't say anything. She just looked down at me. Kinda weird. Confused. It scared me.

I took a long look at her and, of course, I said, "You guessed all along. Just didn't want to admit it to yourself. Didn't you, Lori?"

She didn't say anything. She didn't have to say anything.

I knew all about being twisted. Things her mother had told me. Secrets. How Bill had not been the best of husbands. How he was a mean kind of step-father, a miserable lazy bastard, a no-good bum, but Lori's mom didn't have much recourse back then.

Yet Lori never needed for anything. She always had the clothes, the toys, the best things she needed growing up. A bit spoiled. All those checks from 'the insurance man' she'd remembered had made it possible for her to have nice clothes and go to the best school. It had paid for her college—even though she'd dropped out after the first few months.

Morris Rauch had loved his daughter, and even after so many years apart, he still sent money to Lori's mother to help take care of her.

I said, "You know in your heart I'm not lying."

She didn't reply. She was shocked. Almost frozen.

"He would beat me, Mr. Powers. Bill. Bill, hurt me, told me I was no good. He would make me cry and...and I thought he was my real father and that I was bad and that he didn't love me. I thought...I was no good. That it was all my fault. I believed all his lies."

"I know, but Bill was not your father. Morris is your father. He's a different man, a good man. And you have that goodness from him in you—if you allow it to come out. If you let it overcome the hate."

She stared at me silently.

"And you know something? He loves you very much."

There were tears now and she tried to hide them. It was soon impossible to stem the tide. She nodded, began crying, letting it all out.

I said, "He helped raise you, from a distance, the only way he was allowed to. He didn't have to do it, he could have walked away, but he loved his daughter. It was hard in those days, a Jewish man, an Irish Catholic woman, with their strict families. It was very difficult, but they're together now. Your mother and Morris love each other and they both love you very much."

She was quiet.

I said, "He's Jewish."

I saw her cringe a bit.

"And that makes you Jewish, too. Not legally, according to their religious law, but morally. You're a Jew too, Lori."

She stared at me like I'd called her the worst name you could call a person. Then she sighed and just nodded, resigned to it all.

I smiled at her, "It's not a disease."

She looked at me almost as if it was. "You said you had proof."

My mind jumped back to what I'd told her earlier.

"Yeah. Papers."

"Where?"

"In my jacket pocket."

"What jacket?"

"I was holding a green jacket when you saw me in the foyer outside of the main room yesterday. The papers are in that jacket. I hung it on the rack with all the other jackets out in the foyer."

She thought about that for a moment.

She said, "You're in bad trouble."

The fucking understatement of the year, but I said, "I need you to help me. We both have to get away from here."

She hadn't thought that far ahead yet. She might help me, but she wasn't thinking of herself. If she did help me escape she'd better damn well think of herself and escape too, before Burk and her friends found out.

Lori left me alone. I didn't know what to make of her. Just what the hell was going on in that twisted head of hers. A mind which I had just helped to twist a few more considerable turns.

* * * * * * *

Time went by and things started heating up outside. I could hear a lot of it. There was a lot of noise and activity on the grounds of the country club. And it wasn't golfers pairing up to do a quick nine holes either.

I could make out some things through a slit in the wooden wall behind me and it didn't sound encouraging. Guards and dogs prowled every foot of the grounds now, and there was a lot of commotion and military-style movement. Then late in the morning limousines began coming into the compound and soon after that, helicopters began landing on the flat hill behind the main hall and I knew that there was serious shit brewing.

This wasn't just a meeting of a bunch of the local Nazi-Aryan-Klan groups I'd seen Thursday night with Burk. This was something more. Bigger. Much bigger. Something much more serious and dangerous. Maybe even, something that might bring America to its knees? I felt a horrible chill run through me. I knew that I had to find out just what the hell was going on.

Lori came back a few hours later. She was dressed back in her Nazi-bitch best but I could tell that while her body was in that uniform, her heart wasn't any longer. Her heart just wasn't in it.

She said, "It's too dangerous now. They're all here, from all over, but maybe it might be the best time, too."

I didn't know what she was talking about.

I didn't care either, because I brightened when I saw her pull out a couple of keys and watched with relief as she undid the shackles and chains that bound me.

She said, "Keep them on, make it look like you're still a prisoner. I'll call the guards and we'll take them out, get their weapons, and get out of here."

It was going too fast, that was good, but I still had to find out. "What's going on here, Lori? Who are all the people that have been coming here all day?"

She stopped. "We can't talk about it now, it's much too dangerous."

"I know, but I have to know what's going on," I said.

"A meeting. It's like...Burk somehow got it all worked out...it's amazing...all the groups...all kinds...the hardcore, the leaders, the Klan, Crips, Bloods, BTK, BLA, FOI, Yahwahs, Mafia, Hezbollah and Hamas terrorist cells, Asian Tongs and Triads, Jamaican Posses, old guard sixties Commie terrorists, The Black Barons, Aryan Nation, contingents from Elohim City, others...so many...."

"In other words, this psycho creep has gathered together the leaders of every fucking hate group, criminal enterprise and underground anti-American terrorist cell in the United States?" I asked, stunned.

"Yeah," she said, "pretty amazing, huh?"

Now I really shuddered.

"For what purpose?" I asked.

Lori looked at me with that, 'We really gotta get outta here' look, but I just said, "Come on, Lori! What are they planning?"

She shrugged. "To...you know? Work together. Arthur Burk has figured some way to get to them, to make all the leaders agree to work together."

I swallowed hard. "To do what?"

She looked at me. Incredulous. "Work together."

"To do what, Lori?" I repeated.

"What the hell do you think? To take over! To break down

the country. Right now they're parceling out areas of control, spheres of influence Arthur likes to call them, certain cities and certain states will go to each group. To do with as they please."

I shivered. It was actually happening.

Arthur Burk and leaders from a hundred violent hate groups and crime organizations were ready to join forces to make war and cut up my country into their own private fiefdoms. It was something that could never be done by one group alone, but if united, even for a little while, operating all at once, coordinating their actions, then they could make the country scream. Bleed. Maybe even, fall. The resulting mess would have everyone at each other's throats, then they would pick up the pieces.

"Now come on," Lori insisted. "We have to get away."

I said, "We have to stop it, Lori. We have to find a way to stop them."

"Are you crazy! Do you know who you're dealing with!"

"That's exactly the reason why they have to be stopped." I said.

"Yeah, call the cops!" She smiled, "You know how many of them are here? Cops, I mean?"

I nodded.

"We have to get out of here first," Lori said. She was scared now, and with good reason, my words were making her nervous. So was I. She told me to get ready, then she called in the two guards stationed outside.

The door opened and two Aryan biker types with Chinese Red Army AK47s entered. Lori was on them in a moment and before I could do anything she had them both down and out. She passed me one of the AK47s and took the other. Then she quickly gagged and tied up the two guards.

Afterwards I said to Lori, "My jacket? Is it still...?"

"I never went to check the papers. I guess I knew all along you were telling me the truth and...."

"Forget about that. Where's the jacket?"

"I don't know, I guess it's where you left it."

"I've got to see what's going on here, and I've got to get that jacket back!"

"Vic, you're crazy. Leave the damn jacket! Let's just get out of here!"

"No, you don't understand." I put down the AK47, picked up the chains wrapping them around me so that it looked like I was a bound prisoner again. "You're going to get me into that main hall. I want to see what's going on in there. First-hand. And if what's going on there is what I think it is, I want that jacket and what's in it real bad."

She didn't get me, but that was okay. She took me at gunpoint from the outbuilding, across the compound loaded with people, over to the steps of the main hall.

The compound area was flooded with lights, vehicles, men, women, growling pit bulls, all types of creeps all over the place and each one heavily loaded down with weapons of all kinds. There were six guards at the entrance hall. They wore full *Totenkoff* Death's Head SS regalia. They looked it. Killers. Ready. Just waiting for the word.

Lori walked me through them with a "Heil Hitler" and a Nazi salute, then on into the inner foyer, turning down assistance from the guards to handle her prisoner. She was still security chief and had proven her prowess to these men on numerous occasions, just as she had proven it to me by dispatching the two guards at my cell so recently.

* * * * * * *

Once in the foyer there were two more guards standing in front of the large oak doors that lead into the huge main room. My destination.

Lori sent these two guards away on some pretext and for the moment the two of us were alone.

"We won't have much time," she said. "They'll be back soon."

Then I saw my green jacket. It was just where I had left it on a hook on the coat rack with a hundred other coats and jackets. I picked it up, quickly checked the pocket for my little toy.

It was still there.

I moved over to the huge oak doors of the main hall.

There was a small slit between the two doors and I could just barely get a glimpse into the room. What I saw there sent a chill down my back that I'll never forget. All around a huge table sat the leaders of every hate group and crime organization, terrorist cell, and drug gang in the country. All colors, all creeds, all types—all of them! Together! I recognized a few of them from the TV news. There must have been a hundred leaders, and behind them were their lackeys, body guards, their flags and emblems; everything from Nazi *Swastika* flags to flags of Hezbollah, Aryan Nation, Fruit of Islam, Black Liberation Army, Yahwahs, Crips, *La Cosa Nostra*, Columbian Cartel families, Mexican drug Lord Generalissimo's, and a hundred others. A United Nations of hate. One leader for each group or organization, a nest of the worst vipers and parasitical maggots of hatred this country has ever produced. All colors, all races, all ideologies. Extreme right wing, extreme left wing, extreme center middle-class back-to-the-1950s authoritarian assholes. And all of them armed to the teeth with weapons.

Arthur Burk rose to speak, a blood red swastika flag draped behind him, the various leaders quiet, but each one looking to him now. Expectantly.

He said, "We are not friends, but we do share common goals. Let us always keep that in mind and we shall see those goals accomplished."

There were nods of approval all around.

"We all hate America—for our own reasons—and we seek to carve out a place here for our own identity and destiny from the ashes of this repressive, corrupt, and weak dying nation. If there is something else we can all agree on here tonight, it is that we all want to make America bleed!"

There were cheers. I almost burst a blood vessel listening to it. Knowing what it meant. All the innocents these maniacs would murder, the women, the children, but none of that mattered to these monsters.

Burk continued, emboldened by the support, "Now we all know what we have to do, each of our groups will begin action at the pre-arranged and agreed upon time. According to schedule. The plan cannot fail. The government cannot stand up to all of us, everywhere, at the same time. Imagine, what they are up against, not just one Oklahoma City, but one hundred! They will not even understand the enormity of what has happened until it is too late. And by then, our various groups will have consolidated control in our respective areas, to begin the carving of America that we shall remake into our own image. It is time. The time for violence is now! Violence is the only solution!"

I'd seen enough. "We have to get away from here fast!"

I told Lori.

She didn't argue, she'd been trying like hell to get me to leave since we left the storage shack where I'd been imprisoned.

* * * * * * *

I pressed the button on the tiny electronic timing device in my jacket pocket. The detonator was armed and running. We had thirty minutes and then half the wilderness of the state of New Jersey was going to explode into an inferno of thunder and flames and wholesale death. Or so I hoped.

On the way out across the compound Lori and I passed the soldiers and bodyguards of many of the groups present: black and white racists, crime orgs, gangs, commie-America-hating-traitors, and right wing mutants, religious nuts with guns, dreadlocked freaks with Cuban weapons, Nambla scum, killers for hire from the IRA, human bombs from Hamas, crooked FBI and ATF weasels, shitbag moron losers and lowlifes, all openly boasting about how they were going to kill all the people they didn't like. Get back at the ones they wanted to get back at. Get back at the Blacks. Get back at the whites. Get back at the Jews. Jews who wanted to get back at Arabs. Who were getting back at them. Islam guys who were going to put women back in Purdah, after they killed all the Jews and burned all the churches.... It never ended. Fantasies. Or, would it be worse? Reality? Reality that was just a few hours away from beginning?

Some talked of how they were going to make all the Blacks slaves again, others of how they were going to drive the White Devils into the sea, reopen the ovens for the Jews, wipe out the Mud People, or the Ice People, destroy all the Gays, anyone they hated enough to want to hurt—when the people they really hated the most were themselves. And it made me so sick to see and hear it all, so much hatred, so useless, from so many sides, from every race, every conceivable ideology, all ethnic backgrounds, each ready to destroy the country that had given them so much.

The country I loved.

The country I loved. The country I also knew that was very sick. The country I knew that had problems. But a country that was still the best there ever was—if people would only cool down and give things a chance. But that wasn't in the cards for these monsters. They lived on hate, and planned to go on a spree of murder and genocide the likes of which America had never seen before. Each hate group, each criminal gang, each posse, each drug lord carving up a piece of the American pie to become their own private territory. Their 'sphere of influence' as Arthur Burk had called it, and God help the innocent people unlucky enough to be the 'wrong' people to be caught in the sights of their guns!

With Lori pushing me onward we were able to reach one of the gates at the rear of the country club grounds. Thanks to Lori, we quickly got the jump on the few unwitting guards there, and then headed over the fence and into the pitch-black New Jersey wilderness.

* * * * * * *

The explosion shook the ground like an earthquake, sending shock waves all around us, with a huge fireball hundreds of feet into the night sky. It was an incredible sight, and lit the

Jersey sky for miles. Immediately afterwards there were many smaller explosions, and soon fires grew all around the central compound.

I looked at Lori and she looked at me and I said, "Arthur Burk was right about one thing—violence is the only solution—for people like him."

Lori nodded and ripped off the *swastika* armband throwing it down into the New Jersey mud.

"Let's get out of here, Vic. I want to go home, I miss my Mom, and I have a lot to talk about—with my real father."

I nodded. We kept on moving.

* * * * * *

The TV was on in the background in the Rauch apartment but no one was watching it. Lori was hugging her mother and the two of them were crying.

When Morris Rauch came into the room and saw his daughter I could see the conflict etched in his old face, anger fighting love, sadness and disgust, so many emotions, but the love in him was winning out. It always did with good men like him. He said, "Lori, I'm glad you've come home."

Then Lori and her mother went over to Morris and the three hugged so tight and for so long I thought that they'd break their bones or something and the mother just said, "Now we're a real family."

* * * * * *

I was sitting alone watching the TV news later on when Lori's mother came into the room. They'd all been gone a long time in one of the back rooms having a private talk. I sat down watching a rerun of *Bonanza*. Hoss had found a girl friend and....

"Lori and Morris are talking. They have a lot to talk about."

"I imagine so," I said.

Lori's mother smiled at me. "We shouldn't have kept the

truth from her, but Bill, he was such a rotten bastard and so anti-Semitic, he poisoned her mind.... I thought we were doing a good thing by hiding the truth, but now I know it was the wrong thing...."

I nodded. "It's over now. It's all for the best." I thought of Burk and those scumbags all dead, and said, "It really did turn out for the best."

"Lori is so sorry," her mother told me.

I said, "That's a start."

She nodded quietly. Thoughtful.

* * * * * * *

The TV flicked with bright light. It got our attention. The news was on now and the lead story was being shouted in our faces. The TV newsman saying, "...and a terrible explosion at this prestigious New Jersey Country Club...early indications seem to point to a gas pipeline that burst and was somehow ignited...a national sales conference was underway this weekend...."

She didn't know. I hadn't told her. And I was sure Lori hadn't told her either.

Lori's mother was shocked by the TV news.

"So much violence in the news these days, Mr. Powers...," she said with a helpless sigh.

"Yeah," I said.

The TV newsman continued, "Many bodies have been pulled from the raging fires.... Some weapons were recovered.... Preliminary investigations indicate.... It seems to have been billed as some kind of sales conference, but...anyway, the amount of destruction out here is so devastating that we may never know what really happened."

And Lori's mother said, "My God, such a terrible explosion, Mr. Powers. So many people dead."

I said, "Ah, yeah, too bad."

She looked at me curiously, "Seems strange to me to have weapons at a sales conference though? I wonder what they were selling? Weapons, I guess?"

"Hate," I said.

"Hate, Mr. Powers?"

"They were selling hate, Mrs. Rauch," I said. And I don't think she understood and I didn't feel like explaining it to her. Maybe Lori would tell her one day, but I was too damn sick of it all to talk about it just then.

"They were selling...hate, Mr. Powers?" she continued. I could see her stretching to understand something that she knew I was purposefully not making clear to her. And that I wasn't going to make clear to her. I'd not bring up Lori. I left it at that.

I smiled, said, "Yeah, they were selling hate, but no one's gonna be buying now. They're all dead."

"I don't understand, Mr. Powers," she said.

And I said, "I'm sure you don't, Mrs. Rauch. You and your husband are good people. Good people usually don't understand the lengths to which Evil will go. A fellow recently told me he thought that violence was the only solution to the problems we have in America. But the truth is, violence is never any kind of solution at all...." I smiled, then added, "...except for people like him."

* * * * * * *

I was sitting home alone. Thinking about my city, my state, my country. Things weren't all that good in the good old USA these days but maybe they weren't that bad either. There are problems, but they're workable. I took a deep breath, let it out slow. It's kinda like that. Breathing. Breathing room. It makes things better. Maybe if everyone gave everyone else a chance to breathe, or at least if we tried—made an honest effort—things could be a little bit better. And sometimes just a little bit better can mean a whole lot better.

I was thinking how things were already a lot better in a country without Arthur Burk or any of his ilk left alive in it. You see, America was one hell of a better place already.

Of course, it wasn't over. Months had passed but these things are never over. They're never done especially when you think they're done. They have a life all their own. They just go on, pre-programmed since childhood, passing from one person to the next, like some damn virus. Worse than AIDS, like a bubonic plague of hate.

I got the call from a flatfoot old-timer dick that ran the Seventy-First. He said, "Powers?"

"Yeah?"

"McCready here, remember me?"

"Slow Joe?"

"Don't call me that. I wanna see you. Now! Here. 241 West Street...."

I felt that old chill creeping up on me as my nape hair stood on end.

"What's up?"

"You did some work for the Rauchs a while back?"

"Yes?"

"I want you here. I'm sending a prowl car for you. I want you here. Now."

"What the hell is up?"

"Powers, ah, I don't know. We got a deuce here."

I knew what that meant. Shit! "Who?"

"White male, mid sixties, white female mid fifties."

"What about the kid?" I asked.

"What kid?"

I said, "Forget about sending the car, I'll be right over."

* * * * * * *

McCready met me at the door. I saw them taking out Morris and Mrs. Rauch. I never did remember her first name.

"Double murder? Suicide? What?" I asked.

"You tell me?" McCready insisted.

"I don't know, I did some missing person work for them a few months back. Found their daughter, brought her home. No big deal," I lied.

"We don't know, it looks like a domestic. A bad domestic. The wife and husband fought. Looks like the husband beat her pretty bad, she may have went for his gun, they fought, the gun went off. The husband kills the wife, then turns the gun on himself. Puts one through his temple."

I nodded, "Domestic shit."

"Yeah, looks like it" he replied. "I guess I don't need you here right now. It looks pretty cut and dried."

"Yeah," I said. "Pretty straight forward if you ask me. Guy goes off on his wife."

"Happens all the time, Powers," McCready laughed, he winked at me, "tempted to go off on my old lady a few times myself. That woman can bitch a man to hell!"

I asked him if I could leave and he told me to get the hell out.

* * * * * * *

I was out on the street five blocks away before I shouted, "Fucking bullshit!"

No way Morris killed his wife! No way they fought! She was the love of his life! No way this was any kind of domestic shit.

This was murder!

I'd been played for a fool.

This was Lori.

God Damn her!

* * * * * * *

She was at my place when I got there. Waiting for me. She knew. She was smart. Tying up loose ends.

"Sit down," she said, motioning me to my sofa, with her gun trained on me meaningfully.

I remembered, she knew how to use it.

I sat.

"You did it?" I asked. I don't know why. I knew she did, but I just had to ask. Maybe there was an explanation? A reason? Something?

"Yeah," she admitted. That was all she said.

"Did they have to die?" I asked.

She smiled, her eyes wide, crazy, "They all have to die, Mr. Powers. And so do you."

"You tricked me," I said.

"I'm very good," she said with evident pride. "Arthur Burk was a fool. But useful, up to a point, until he tried to take over. Well, now he's out of my way and I can still go forward with the plan. My plan, Mr. Powers. Delayed a year or so, but all the more potent for that delay when placed into action."

I shook my head. What a fucking mess.

She laughed, "We're a lot alike, Mr. Powers, and I would truly like to speak to you at length, but I don't have a lot of time right now, and you have to die."

"You don't have to kill me?"

She laughed then, said, "Vic, I do like you, but you're such a dickhead."

Then she got up and came over to me. Always letting me know that the gun was there, ready. But she came in close, then closer still, until we were touching. She still held the gun on me, this time hard against my head, while her lips sought out my own lips.

She was some piece of work.

She smiled and I almost wet my pants, then she kissed me, and so help me I grabbed for her throat and just squeezed. She didn't react, just bit my lip, drawing blood. As I squeezed harder, she bit down harder, all the time her tongue reaching down deep into my mouth.

The taste of blood was everywhere.

I was terrified, expecting her to pull the trigger any moment and blow the top of my head away, but it never happened.

Instead I kissed her back, loving her perfect lips, holding her to me tightly with my left hand, as I tried my best to strangle her to death with my right hand.

I squeezed hard, cutting off her breathing, feeling her go cold, blue, scared, like she was getting ready to die.

She still did not pull the trigger of the gun she had to my head.

I never knew why.

She died in my arms.

We never said a word to each other.

I guess that's the way it had to be.

I didn't care.

It was the right thing to do.

Sometimes violence really is the only solution.

You see...*I really do believe in homicide.*

DOGS KNOW

Sometimes I think back on things. When Larry used to be alive. He was the best partner a cop ever had, the only friend I'd ever known. So damn real.

I was always the wild foolish one. Larry was calm, logical, orderly, quiet. He had a good life, loving wife, great kids; he proved it could be done. It was incomprehensible to me, but Larry did it. He made the good things happen.

I wouldn't have stayed a cop if it hadn't been for Larry. I was always in trouble. He would always straighten me out, cool me down. We'd talk a lot, and he'd always give me the best damn advice. Free. Not like a lot of the shitheads that want to latch onto your life or get influence over you. Larry didn't care about that crap. Larry just wanted what was best for his friends and family. To Larry, his friends were family too.

I know what he used to do. Something no one ever does anymore. He used to go outside himself to help a friend. Help his family. I know he considered me family and the thought brought tears to my eyes when I saw him lowered into the ground. He went outside himself for me time and again. No one's ever done that for me before or since. Not friends, not family. Especially not family. All they ever wanted was to drain me dry and throw out what was left—or ignore me. Pretend I was dead. That I didn't exist. That I was nothing. I wanted to go outside myself for Larry now. To show him. I would. Somehow.

I remember the last time I was over Larry's house. It was when he got the dogs. They were monstrous brutes. One was a big German Shepherd, the other two, silk black Dobermans. They were all big as hell and ugly as sin. Larry's dogs meant business.

I don't know where he got them but I know he was training them. They'd make good pets for his boys and protect the house and family when he wasn't home. Being a cop, he wasn't home much. Now he wouldn't be home ever again. The dogs were still there though, to watch over Susan and the boys. Larry saw for the protection of his own.

On that day long ago, the dogs sat quietly watching me as I approached the high chain-link fence Larry had around the house. It was one of those cool spring days, bright sunny mornings. Even the air smelled good. He was doing some junk in the yard. He was always working on the house, worked like a damn dog himself, but never complained. He looked happy as hell when he was working. He waved me in.

I just laughed. "Shit, man! I ain't coming in there! The dogs'll tear me apart."

"Don't worry about them, Vic," he told me with a laugh.

I nodded, "Sure. As long as I'm on *this* side of the fence I won't worry at all."

He just laughed. He was hammering something, making something out of wood for his boys or the neighborhood kids. He always tinkered with stuff.

When he saw I wouldn't budge he got up and came over to the fence. "What's wrong, scared of a few puppies?"

"Yeah, puppies. Suppose they think I'm some slimebag coming to mug you? Rob the house? Steal your tinker toys?"

"Nah, don't worry, they won't hurt you. I'm telling you, Vic, they can pick up on things better than people. Things like feelings, friendship, belonging. You belong, Vic. Believe me, dogs know."

I said, "Fine, Larry, dogs know," but I didn't move until he came out of the gate to where I was standing nice and safe.

It was funny back then. We joked around. Talked a lot. We had dreams. He busted my chops because I was being a peckerhead by fooling with this fast girl that was no good for me but a lot of damn fun all the same. Larry always told me to be careful, keep it in my pants. Fun ain't all there is he'd tell me. I never listened and paid the price. I never could see what else there was beside fun. The other side only seemed to be pain and hurt and I'd seen enough of that.

Self control and clear thinking was Larry's thing. He had it. I never did. That could be why we partnered so well together. It's sure as hell why I lasted on the force for so long after all the crap we saw in the day-to-day.

* * * * * * *

I was real shook when the cop killer got Larry. It bothered me, even though it hadn't been my fault. I mean, I told him not to leave me, not to go after the guy alone—but Larry didn't listen. The one time I was right—he didn't listen to me!

I'd been hit. Leg wound and it was bleeding badly. Larry seemed so calm about it, like usual, so by-the-book. I thought, OK, we're cool, things will be OK. Larry quickly made an improvised tourniquet for my wound, ran back to the car and pulled the shotgun from the trunk.

I didn't know what was happening. I thought he was going to stand guard over me or something until backup arrived. Logical right? The way it should be done. Larry was always so calm, doing the smart thing. Only this time he acted more like *me* than I'd ever done. He saw me hit, bleeding, maybe dying, and he freaked for vengeance.

It all happened so fast. The cop killer had struck once before in this borough. We were in our usual prowl area and were on the lookout for him like everyone else. We never expected to find him. We didn't. He found us. He was hunting cops. The whole thing was a set-up and we'd walked right into it.

"No!" I shouted, "Don't do it!"

"Shut up and stay put," Larry whispered, calm, smiling now, "This won't take long. I'll be back in five minutes."

He slipped two cartridges into the shotgun, then blended into the darkness of the night so damn fast—like between heartbeats.

I tried like hell to get up and follow him. I knew the backups would be here soon, but they'd be too late. I remember crawling across the wet asphalt, moving forward, leaving a sticky smear of red behind me like I was a damn snail. I'd knotted the tourniquet, tied it as tight as I could. It wasn't working so great, too much leakage. So much blood now. I tried to get up on my good leg, stumble, hop, do anything to catch up to Larry. It wouldn't work. By then I was dizzy and much too weak. So I crawled. Crawled like a motherfuckin' bug. My revolver drawn, my eyes searching desperately for Larry in the darkness, searching for the killer, seeing nothing but the blackness of the night. The shadows, the black of the bricks, the asphalt and concrete were all closing in on me.

Finally, I spotted Larry. I was about to yell out to him to get back to the car, when I heard the shots. They came out of the blackness around me, and they struck him down.

* * * * * * *

It was weeks before I recovered. At least physically. Mentally, I don't know. I'm Vic Powers, I got my own way of dealing with things. It's different from most people. Let's leave it at that for now.

It was weeks later when I was able to really move around. The first thing I did was extend my time off. Wounded cop. Line of duty. I got it, no sweat. Then I decided to perform my own investigation and get Larry's killer.

I had some good hunches. Better facts. Facts I had not put in my report. I'd seen the killer. Clear. After he'd shot Larry he came out from his hiding place. He came out to look at his handy work. He stood there. Laughing. It was only for a minute. He didn't know I was there, but I saw his face as clear as daylight in the flash of a headlight from a passing car. That was all I needed. I could wait. I'd never forget that face.

* * * * * * *

Rounding up the creep was no problem. It didn't take me long to dig around and find him. I'm good at that stuff. Once I get the scent I run all the way with it. Hungry. Non-stop.

The piece-of-shit was my meat now. I had him tied and gagged in the trunk of my car. I was driving around the city thinking about what the hell I was going to do to him. There were a lot of possibilities. This was something I wanted to think through real good. It was for Larry.

It was a good feeling to have Larry's killer just where I wanted him. I kept thinking about that. I thought about what Larry would have done. Shit, he'd have done the right thing and brought the guy in.

"I can't do that, Larry," I said out loud. It went against the grain. What if the killer got off from some soft-bellied judge? What if some liberal idiots figure he didn't get as many "rights" as he was entitled to and he got a light, easy sentence? I'd seen that kind of thing happen way too much.

Damn weasels!

That's the bullshit they call justice—but the only justice for a murderer is a quick bullet in the brain and six feet of dirt.

I hung a turn onto the parkway. Floored the gas pedal. The speed felt good and there was no traffic. Speedometer moving up to 60, past 65 now. I popped another upper. Been driving a long time. Thinking. Thinking so much it hurt.

When I finally became aware of the sounds I didn't know what the hell they were. Then I realized, banging from the trunk. The killer was awake, kicking around in the darkness, trying to get out.

"Shut up! You fuckin' murdering bastard!"

He kept kicking. The sound went right through my brain.

I took a sharp turn, I knew that would rattle his cage a bit.

"Now shut up and let me think!"

The banging wouldn't stop. It was driving me crazy.

"Larry what should I do with this piece of garbage?"

Larry wouldn't answer me just then. Maybe it was the drugs. Or me being so tired. I mean, I knew Larry was dead and couldn't talk to me, but I really needed to hear his voice just then. I really needed to talk to him. The fact that we'd never talk again just burned me up. It couldn't be! It just couldn't be! Maybe Larry was dead, but I could still talk to him. I needed to talk to him just then.

"I'm alone, man, help me. I don't know what to do."

The banging began again. Into my brain.

"I need you, Larry. Why'd you leave me? Why'd you put yourself out there to save me? I wasn't worth it!"

The banging continued. Drowning out the sound of the car.

"I'm all alone now, Larry. I don't know what the fuck to do anymore!"

The banging grew louder. Intense.

"Shut up back there! You fuckin' killer! You killed the only friend I ever had! He was like a brother to me and you killed him for no damn reason!"

The killer tried to yell but the tape over his mouth made only tiny sounds. But I heard them. I heard them! *I HEARD THEM!*

"Shut up! I'll stop this car right now and rip your fuckin' face off with my damn hands if you don't shut up!"

The kicking stopped. The noise stopped.

OK, that was better. I tried to open another bottle of beer. Finally got it open and chugged it down between the tears. Threw the empty in the back seat. It shattered on another bottle. I didn't care.

The guy was quiet now. Now I could think. So I drove around the city. Thinking. Talking with Larry's ghost in the passenger seat beside me like the old days. Trying to figure out what we should do.

I thought about how lovely it was going to be to plug that murdering son-of-a-bitch. Plug him real good. Permanent customize job on that fucker. But it had to be good. It had to be special. Just killing him wasn't enough. It had to mean something, just as Larry's life had meant something. So much.

"What should I do, Larry?" the highway lights rushing over my tearful eyes, fogging my glassy vision, leaving me alone and confused. "Why'd you leave me! I'm so lost now. I don't know what the hell to do. Help me, Larry!"

I knew it had to be the drugs talking. I didn't care. Before I crashed I popped some more uppers, letting the car drive me. We drove all over. It eventually took me to the old neighborhood, the place where Larry and I had grown up. I don't know how I got there but it was significant. It was the place where Larry had chosen to live his life with Susan and raise their family. I knew then that Larry was guiding my hand.

I passed the house slowly. Everything looked the same; nothing seemed to have changed since the killing. Except for Larry. He was gone now forever. The feeling of loss was heavy in the air, like a thick fog swirling all around me, everything so sad, so lonely. I could feel what Susan and the boys were going through. Susan's quiet determination, her bravery, the sadness, that cold loneliness in bed at night as she slept alone. Without Larry for the rest of her life. That was an aching loss that would always be an open wound. Then there was the anger of the boys; all they'd miss growing up without a father. And Larry was a *great* father! Just when they'd really need him—he couldn't be there for them. I knew what they felt. I felt it too.

My fist smashed the dashboard.

I stopped the damn car.

I knew what I had to do now.

* * * * * *

It was dark. Just right for what I'd decided. I parked the car. It was a quiet street. No one was around. I unlocked the truck and took out the garbage.

"If you make one move, one whisper, I'll blow your fuckin' brains out. Got it!"

He nodded, shivering, eyes ablaze.

He was cuffed, hands behind, duct tape over the mouth. I cut off another piece of tape. A long piece. Wrapped it around his head so it covered his eyes. Tight. He wasn't seeing nothing.

"We're going for a walk, don't give me no problems."

I pulled him out of the trunk and he fell to the asphalt. I pulled him to his feet by his hair. I took my right hand and dug it into the back of his neck leading him forward. To the gate. I saw the doghouse Larry had built for the three monsters. The three monsters weren't anywhere in sight. I knew Susan kept them in the house since the murder. It helped having them around, helped with the loneliness. They were Larry's dogs and he loved them, a small part of Larry left alive in the world. The dogs were a part of the family; they were Larry's children too. They were the boys' brothers now.

I opened the gate to the backyard. It slid open silently. I pushed the killer forward.

There was a metal pole in the center of the yard. It was about twenty feet high, made of thick gauge piping Larry had cemented into the ground. It was real solid. Larry was going to make an old time swing or something for him and Susan someday. That day would never come now but I hoped to put it to good use. I pushed the killer to the ground, unlocked one of the cuffs, quickly putting it back on again with his arms behind the pole. I left the tape on his mouth and eyes.

He got nervous and tried to kick me almost hitting my sore leg. I smacked him upside the head. He bled a bit, was stunned. I held myself back from finishing the job.

I left him there and went to the house, rang the bell.

Susan answered. Behind her were Larry's four teenage sons, the three dogs stood strangely quiet in the background. Waiting. Anticipating. Watching so damn interested.

Susan was surprised. "Vic? What are you doing here?"

I said, "Susan, I've got something for you, for the boys. Something for Larry too. He's chained in the back yard. It's the man who killed Larry. I saw him do it. He's yours. Do whatever you want to him. No one need ever know. I'll be back this time tomorrow night to take care of what's left."

Then I left. Their faces blank, stunned. None of them knew what to say. Neither did I. I'd said enough. I got in my car and drove away.

* * * * * * *

I drove around for hours. Thinking things through. Trying to figure it out in my own way. Why did this guy want to kill cops? Not one particular cop, just any cop. I couldn't figure it. Maybe he didn't even know why he did it? He just did it. I didn't care now. He'd murdered Larry and that was enough for me. It didn't have to make sense. Not everything makes sense. Damn little really does anymore. To me.

I didn't know what Susan and the boys would do to him. I figure they deserved the opportunity to make him pay, they were owed that much, at least. Hey, isn't that what America's all about? Opportunity. And Justice! Let the family decide what the killer deserved.

I know it was a stupid thing to do. Not only career-wise. Hell, my cop career was going right down the toilet since Larry's death. I knew that. I didn't care now. I'd never be able to handle it again. Not that I did so well before. And now, the more I thought about it, I realized I'd messed up again. Real bad. I'd put Susan and the boys in terrible jeopardy, made them have to make nasty choices they should have been spared. I'd also placed them in considerable danger. What if that bastard got loose? It would be on my head. If he didn't get away, then Larry's boys would just tear the bastard apart. They weren't so much like their dad, but they loved him fiercely. They'd destroy the guy who murdered him if they could. I'd made that possible now. And it might destroy them if they did it and word got out.

"I'm such a stupid shit! Why do I always fuck up the worst when I try to do good?"

I looked at my watch. It was already five a.m. I'd been driving most of the night. I hadn't slept in two days. I was running on coffee and uppers. And beer. Where the hell was I anyway? I had to hurry. I hit traffic on the way back. By the time I got into Brooklyn it was already rush hour.

I was nervous. Flying from the pills and lack of sleep. Worried about what I'd find in the back yard. Susan and the boys had been through so much, now I'd put this shit on them. I felt like crap.

I pulled up to the house with a screech, got out of the car, ran to the front porch. Susan opened the door. She was alone; the boys were probably on the way to school that time of morning. Or were they out in the back carving up the killer!

Susan saw me but didn't say a word.

"Susan...?"

She shook her head. Stunned.

"Is he dead?" I asked.

She ignored my question. There was fierce anger in her face.

"Vic, we had a very bad night last night because of you."

"Sue, I know. I'm so sorry, I wasn't thinking right...."

"The boys went wild. I lost control over them for the first time. I thought they were going to kill that bastard, tear him apart, but they didn't. It was so weird, Vic, it wasn't like they didn't want to do it, even I thought about it last night when I was alone in bed. Alone in the bed Larry and I used to share. But the boys stopped. They were really going to kill him—but they stopped."

"I'm glad, Sue. I'll go get him and bring him in."

"Vic, that was such a stupid thing to do," but she gave me a sad little smile as she said it, "but we all love you for it. Don't think we don't understand. I wish it could have brought Larry back, and if it would have, I would be the first one to pull the trigger on that piece of filth, but please, Vic, get that garbage out of our back yard. Take it where it belongs. I don't want his presence fouling our house anymore."

I nodded. A bit subdued for once. She slowly closed the door, looking so tired. I went to the side of the house, though the gate, out to the back yard.

The killer, his name wasn't important, was right where I'd left him the night before. Same position. Same condition. Untouched. His mouth and eyes were still covered with the duct tape. His hands still cuffed behind him to the pole. He lay stretched out, quiet, motionless.

I moved up close. He stiffened. I whispered into his ear.

"So no one touched you. You're a lucky piece-of-shit! These are good people, you don't deserve their mercy. I'm taking you in for the murder of policeman Larry Jenkins. I saw you do it. I'm his partner, the one you wounded in the leg. The one that didn't die."

I moved behind him and bent down low to put my key into the left cuff. It snapped open. He lashed out with his leg, his boot smashing into my bad leg. His wrist slid out of the cuff. I let out a gasp of pain. He let loose with a roundhouse swing, the metal cuff catching me square on the side of the head near the eye. I reeled, fell back stunned, seeing stars for a moment. By the time I could see images again, the killer had ripped the duct tape off his eyes and mouth and was on me like a madman.

He knew I was the only thing between him and freedom. I was the only witness. Take me out and no one would ever know. He wasn't a big guy, normally I could have smashed him a dozen ways to Sunday, but he was wiry and frantic, and his attack had me off balance. I was having trouble fighting him off, seeing two of him, four hands at my throat pressing tighter and tighter. I tried to shake him off, but he was good, and I knew I was in a fight for my life with a killer who had everything to gain by my death and nothing to lose.

I tried to reach inside my jacket to get at my revolver, but it wasn't there. Then he hit me again. Hard. Two, three times. It was hard to think straight anymore, the hands at my throat were cutting off my breathing. Things started to get fuzzy all around me. I felt the killer's fingers digging deeper and deeper into my throat, my corded muscles slowly giving way as he pressed, cutting off my breathing.

I remember seeing his face up so close. Young, almost handsome, now all twisted with hatred and bloodlust. The son-of-a-bitch was smiling, he knew what was coming, soon he was going to add one more dead cop to his tally.

My head lolled over to the side, I tried to hit him, knock him off me, but my fists could only hit weak and glancing blows that hardly seemed to bother him.

I saw Susan at the screen door on the back porch. Her attention had finally been drawn by the noise of the fight. The alarm in her face said it all to me, she knew I was a goner too.

Then Susan opened the screen door.

My voice was able to let out one tiny gasp of terror as I saw Larry's pack of monstrous dogs charging down at me. They ran like bats out of hell. The giant Shepherd with slavering jaws and long razor teeth, the two silk-black Doberman's, eyes ablaze with the killing lust. They were on us instantly. They were on the killer like white on rice. And they held onto him while he screamed. No matter what he did, he couldn't get away, he couldn't shake them off. It was wonderful.

They left me alone, coming real close but not touching me at all, they were only after my attacker. Somehow they knew the difference. They took a chunk of him here, a bite there, drawing blood in a dozen places, moving in on his neck, chomping on his hands as he tried vainly to defend himself. I was able to roll away, watching the dogs close in on the killer's throat, cutting it with bloody teeth, crushing it with jaws that could deliver over 500 pounds of smashing, killing, demolition pressure.

Susan came out of nowhere, muttered a command, the dogs quickly moved off to sit quietly behind her.

I prodded part of the bloody carcass of Larry's killer with my hand. There wasn't much left in one piece and it was obvious he was deader than hell. That pile of garbage never looked so good.

Susan helped me up. I was really shaky, covered in blood, but I didn't care because all of it was the killer's. That was OK by me, he wouldn't need it anymore. It would wash off real easy too.

I watched the dogs. Growing a little nervous, they were watching me so closely. Guardedly. They looked like they were ready for some more action. That's not what I wanted to see.

Susan smiled at me, "What a mess."

"Just what he deserves," I said.

"Not him, Vic. You. And don't be scared of the puppies. It's OK now."

Puppies, I thought. When I found my voice I said, "They make me nervous."

"You make them nervous too, but don't let them bother you."

"I know, that's what Larry always used to tell me."

She smiled at the mention of Larry's name. So did I. We both missed him, both felt him with us just then. I swear, he was there. Smiling.

She said, "The dog's won't hurt you, Vic. They only hurt the enemy. You're not the enemy. Larry was right. Dogs know."

I didn't say a word. Larry was right. Dogs know.

So I tried to pet one of the ugly brutes. He took a snap at my hand, almost taking it off!

Susan laughed. "Larry always said dogs know, Vic. He didn't say they were freakin' geniuses!"

BLACK VOMIT

When José told me he'd seen Rico I didn't buy it. Rico was MIA, lost in Vietnam, but José said it was Rico sure as there's a Hell and that I should come quick and take a look.

I said okay.

When I got to the flea-bag motel on the West Side I looked in on a guy laying on a pile of rags in a stinking corner of a stinking room, coughing his chest out, the place smelling of piss, shit and a dozen other worse odors. I moved close. I looked down at the guy carefully.

It was Rico!

I could hardly believe it. He was in a bad way. He was sick and he was dying, and he was throwing up chunks of dark matter.

José told me he thought Rico had a mighty case of food poisoning, but he'd never seen anything like this before. I knew it couldn't be food poisoning at all.

It knew it for what it was. In Central and South America they call it *Vómito Negro*, we call it Black Vomit. It happens sometimes in the worst cases of the last stages of untreated Yellow Fever. Just before you die, you puke up these dark evil-looking chunks of congealed blood, pus, bile and mucus. It's terrible to see. There's an odor of death about it, the sickly sweet odor of the dark green of infection.

Black Vomit.

* * * * * * *

My memory was going back now, my mind seeing it all the way it used to be in the faraway old days. Rico had been a wild-ass young kid, like we all were back then. Drinking and doping and carousing to all hours with some of the chicks that hung with us. Those had been sweet days for sure. We were all young and strong, and thinking we were kicking the ass of the world. And damn well doing it too, for a short time. Or at least we thought so. Pretty damn stupid too, now that I think back on it. We all had that *we-didn't-care* stupid—that *it-won't-happen-to-me* blindness that the young have. Doing crazy, wild, stupid things and never figuring that you could die from them. You can get away with it sometimes, for a short while when you're young and fast and strong—and if you're real lucky. But only for a few years. Then when it catches up with you—and it sure as hell always will—it'll hit you like a hammer.

Bang!

The hammer that hit a lot of us back in 1968 was a thing called Vietnam. Nobody figured it could really be as bad as it was. No one figured a lot of shit back then. It was like everyone was asleep at the wheel. The car—like our country—driving out of control, plowing on indiscriminately, without any focus or goal, no sense of direction, no rhyme or reason.

After the war too many of us came back like humpty-dumpty people, cracked and broken, some of us all bent out of shape, never being able to put ourselves back together again.

It took me a long time to get straight. Sort of. It didn't last long. I tried to kick the drugs. Get a real job. I became a cop and tried to scrape a life out of the debris of a past full of pain and hopelessness. It worked for a while but then everything fell apart. That's the way it's always been for me. Just when I feel I'm getting on top, I find myself covered by the shit pile. Many of my buddies never came back at all. Some came back, but only physically, their minds still trapped somewhere in the jungle.

Then there were the MIA's.

Over two thousand.

Gone.

Disappeared with no accounting for.

Like the damn Earth had just opened up and swallowed them all.

Over two thousand guys!

That many people just don't disappear. Not without some reason.

* * * * * * *

A lot of it was Charlie, of course. The Communists took a lot of prisoners and killed hundreds of them. Butchered them in cold blood. Torture. Slave labor camps. Public executions. Who knows what happened to the ones that were left? The media covered up too much of it, were denied access, made excuses for the enemy, or just didn't want to notice inconvenient things like facts and truth back then. It interfered with the news story against the way and against our troops. I mean, when has the media ever let the facts get in the way of a story they wanted to tell?

The media didn't want to report anything that might upset the American people—oh sure, stories of the massacre at My Lai or napalming Vietnamese (all innocent, the way they tell it) were fine and dandy—but when it came to the truth about our POW's, about our MIA's, the media didn't want to report anything that might wake up the American people, anything that might make them righteously indignant like Pearl Harbor or the Bataan Death March had done in a past war. That might make America demand and expend serious effort to actually win the damn thing, or to get out quick. Instead of playing the bullshit game being played over there. That kind of crap might even change the military leadership of the war. The very direction the war was taking. It might even change the government of the country!

The media's dirty little secret was that they loved the war. After all, it was their most compelling story; blood and guts brought into every American living room every single night.

Others in the media loved it because it served their own rotten agenda of slamming America as the bad guy. Every single chance they got. And they took it. Boy, did they take advantage!

Vietnam was the war America was not allowed to win, and we've been paying the price for decades now and it looks like the memories and nightmares will never fade. But the worst memory of all was the MIA's. Some of our finest, left behind when the war ended—imprisoned, tortured, killed by the NVA and Communist political commissars in Hanoi prisons and death camps. Others held in secret locations in the jungle. Camps the American people never knew about because sympathizers and conspirators from both political parties in our own government kept the truth secret. Government officials and their media lackeys sugar-coated the stark truth, while others who played the "so-called socially conscious citizen" like Hanoi Jane, went on TV and sold out their fellow countrymen with boldfaced lies and treason. But the worst kind of traitors—the people who sold out our soldiers, our POW's, especially our MIA's, were—our own politicians.

We all knew, even back then, they'd sell their own mother for a vote. What the hell did they give a rat's ass about a lot of kids they didn't even know. Kids unlucky enough to get themselves caught in the meat grinder by an enemy thousands of miles away from home in Vietnam. Were any of them the sons of the rich? The politically connected? Relatives of congressmen, senators, governors, or the President? I don't think so. And if they were, those people got "special assignments"—like Dan Quayle and Al Gore. Sure, they're from different political parties, but isn't it really all the same political party when it comes down to the privileged, elite class? Whether they went to 'Nam or not?

And I don't need to mention people who organized anti-American demonstrations in foreign countries, do I?

* * * * * * *

Well, that was then, this is now. Today the guy I was looking at was a miserable excuse for what was left of a human being. But it was Rico, all right. I could hardly believe it. It was like he was back from the dead—and it looked like he would be back *with* the dead real soon by the looks of him.

I held him in my arms, brushed the long, dirty black hair out of his eyes—eyes that tried furiously to focus on me, dark yellow surrounding dead irises and dilated pupils.

"Vic? Is that you, Vic?"

"Yeah, buddy, it's me."

He gave a short twisted smile and coughed.

I said, "I thought you were lost, Rico. MIA. What happened?"

Rico began a laugh that quickly evolved into a long wracking cough. I held him steady. He smiled up at me, his big mouth full of broken black teeth.

"I'm dying, brother."

He coughed up more blood, dark viscous chunks, white phlegm. It stunk bad.

He motioned me closer. His dry, blood-caked lips brushing against my ear.

"I got something...to tell you, Vic. There were still a handful... left."

"A handful of what, Rico?"

"Americans, Vic. They were still...over there."

Then Rico told me his story: about how he'd deserted in a fire fight in 1972, went underground and later joined a small group of renegade CIA and other military types, some ARVN, a retired U.S. general, even some NVA, and others. The others were guys like Rico, deserters who were listed as MIA on the books. Some had run away and were hiding. Some were with drug dealers. Some had even joined the enemy. In time, these individuals joined with an underground drug-dealing cartel that was bringing heroin into the U.S. from China and Vietnam. Nothing I didn't know. Nothing a lot of people in law enforcement and the media didn't know as well. A lot of Chinese street gangs were organized in the 1970s as U.S. distributors for this kind of trade. But Rico told me that in their dealings with the communist Vietnamese after their victory over the South in 1975—they'd heard hints and stories, seen incriminating evidence, heard Vietnamese soldiers mention "Americans"—not knowing one of the American drug dealers knew their language and could understand what they were saying. Rico told me that up until 1980 there were still Americans alive and held prisoner in Laos. They were still alive back then. Still held prisoner. Sold out, lost, and all but forgotten.

* * * * * * *

Rico died in my arms telling me all the Americans were now dead, butchered in 1980 by communist troops before Reagan became president, murdered in the Laotian jungle, then dumped into unmarked common graves.

Over 500 of them!

Rico said if I wanted to find out more about it...and then he stopped, looked up at me with a strange smile, and then died in my arms.

I mourned him like a long-lost brother. A brother in my arms, and a brother-in-arms.

* * * * * * *

It was the next day when the guy from the CIA came to see me at the run-down hole I was using as an office. I was private dicking back then and figured at first when he walked in, hey, look at this—I got a client! And a damn rich, fancy-suited one at that! Then the antenna went up and I knew he had to be a government man, I smelled some kind of cop all over him and when he stabbed his I.D. in my face I sighed and waited for the other shoe to drop. Figuring, as these things usually happen, that other shoe would soon be finding its way into my unprotected buttocks.

"Name's Derrick Johnson, out of the D.C. office, Mr. Powers. Heard you were an old-time friend of Rico González. Served with him in The 'Nam. You know where he might be?"

I looked him over as he sat down in a chair opposite my desk, looking for all the world like a big fat black Buddha with snake eyes and a killer smile. Sipping on a glass of my booze he'd taken out of my cabinet, eyeing me with the same scrutiny that I was eyeing him—daring me to be stupid or talk shit.

"Rico's dead. He was killed in 'Nam. Back in 1972, I think."

"That is the official line, Mr. Powers, but the company line is that Rico was one of our boys working on something tight. Now we can't find him. You know what I mean."

It wasn't a question, just a statement and one I didn't like. I didn't know what he knew I knew. In fact, I knew I really didn't know much of anything at all, so I didn't know what to tell him just then. Pretty screwed up, if you ask me. And then I thought of José. And I knew for sure that the man in front of me knew a lot of stuff he wasn't letting on.

"All right, I was called by a guy I know to a flea-bitten dive on the West Side late last night to see another guy. It was Rico. He was in bad shape and died just as I got there. He was very sick, untreated Yellow Fever, I think. I seen it before. If you don't get it treated it can kill you and it can be a very nasty way to go. I hardly recognized him at first. We'd been buddies in 'Nam, but I hadn't heard from him in twenty years."

"What did he tell you, Mr. Powers?" Johnson said, filling up his glass again but too busy watching me to actually drink any of my cheap booze.

I knew I was in a bind. They wanted to know how much I knew about the cartel, and probably about the dead American MIA's. Meanwhile I wanted to know just who the hell Johnson really was. Which side was he on?

I decided the best way to find out was to ask him.

Johnson just laughed, "It doesn't really matter, Mr. Powers. You'd never believe me if I told you I was one of the good guys, and if I was lying you wouldn't find out until it was too late. But why not look at it this way: the very fact that you're alive and sucking air this morning should give you a hint that I'm wearing a white hat."

Of course he wasn't wearing a white hat at all. It was all wise-guy metaphorical bullshit talk, like the kind of two-bit philosophical crap mobsters spout about morals and respect and all that honor stuff before they whack some poor slob in cold blood so they can justify to themselves that they did it for some high-minded reason. I knew the kind, but knowing them and dealing with them are two different things. Rico was dead, I figured I'd tell the truth and get rid of this guy. Give him just enough to whet his whistle, but not enough to let on just how much I really knew.

So I said, "You know, you could also be a smart guy who holds off on killing me until after I talk. You could always take me out later today. Tomorrow. Even next week."

He smiled, "Yes, there is always that to consider."

"And I know, you already know that I know about the renegade CIA guys. You can tell that from my reaction to you and your questions."

"That's true, usually we don't have to go through all this bullshit with people. The patriotic ones, or the merely jealous, tell us what they know and are happy to do it. With Communists, Socialists, leftist loonies, they get all indignant and start shouting about the imperialistic, capitalistic, elitist, power structure and all kinds of commie dogma, crap that's in keeping with their warped politically-insane slant on the Company. And so-called liberals, they're the worst! Always so damn guilty about *every-damn-thing*, crying about the rights of every killer creep, Wall Street weasel, whore politician and pervo degenerate and how *their* country has been taken over by the far Right."

I smiled.

"Precisely, just so much crap. But you don't fall into either case, Mr. Powers. You fall into a category that's far different— you fall into the category of someone who knows something. Something far more than just a bunch of words or facts strung together. I think you know the real meaning...of things."

Sweat trickled down my face.

So I spilled my guts and hoped for the best. In the final analysis there wasn't much to tell. In truth, Rico had died before he'd gotten to the punch line of his speech or message or whatever it was he had wanted to tell me. It bugged me no end, but it also probably kept Johnson from digging his claws into my back about what I knew. I really didn't know that much. And I think he realized that. But I did have some hunches.

*　*　*　*　*　*　*

The night passed quietly, me sleeping alone like usual in my hovel of a room, the door and windows sealed shut with makeshift alarms.

I woke the next morning with my head sore from sleeping on a thin pillow with my .45 beneath it. But I had survived the night, and I survived the next. In the meantime I tried to piece it all together.

What weirded me out was when I couldn't find José around any of the neighborhood bars. People said he'd gone off to A.C. to try his luck at the new Trump casino but I wondered where the hell José had gotten the bread to try his luck with. I scanned all the papers for the next couple of days for news of Rico's death. For a funeral notice. Anything. It was like he'd been sucked right back into that huge void he'd fallen into back in 1972. No news of Rico or anyone fitting his description, no body, no funeral, no report, nothing.

A couple of days later I took the shuttle to D.C. to have a chat with Johnson. I had some considerable trouble finding the man and when I did it took a lot of crap to get past the layers of CIA bureaucracy to arrange a meet. Finally Derrick Johnson came out to meet me. Not what I expected at all.

This Derrick Johnson was a tall, skinny, *white* guy!

My Derrick Johnson had been a short, fat, Buddha-like, *black* guy!

I couldn't figure the discrepancy nor accept the fact that the

CIA were *that* good at disguise.

We sat down. We introduced ourselves. I told him my name was Rod. Rod Carew. Yeah, just like the baseball player. I had papers and I.D. I'd shown his people, I even showed him a valid New Jersey driver's license with my photo on it. He laughed a bit about it good naturedly, like he knew the game so well. So did I. I told him I got that kind of reaction all the time. He said he was sure that I did.

We chatted mostly about baseball. About my name and the real Rod Carew. I had no other I.D. on me. For all he knew I really was some guy named Rod Carew, but of course he wasn't buying it for a second and I didn't expect him to either. He did like the name though, gave me the feeling it was, if nothing else, original and witty. I got the impression he was a true baseball fan and liked the respect I was showing—in my own twisted way, of course—to one of the true forgotten greats of the game. I asked him if he was the only Derrick Johnson in the Washington office.

He said he was the only Derrick Johnson in the *entire* CIA.

I told him I must have made a mistake.

He said it seemed likely.

I thanked him and left.

He didn't believe me for a minute.

I lost the tail they put on me when I went into the subway. Then I lay low until dark. That night I stole a car parked on Vermont Avenue and drove back to NYC.

* * * * * * *

I was laying low in a cockroach hotel on the West Side, hookers and short-stay rates, gay boys and TV whores, drug dealers, drug buyers, no questions asked, and every other kind of scoundrel you ever saw. It was the human supermarket.

I thought of Rico. I went to the library and got all the books I could find on Malaria and Yellow Fever. The two diseases are very different, but similar in some ways. They are both deadly to man, both are carried by mosquitoes; but Malaria is caused by a parasite, Yellow Fever by a virus. Quinine has been used for a hundred years to treat victims of Malaria with much success; today there are more potent drugs. There is a vaccine for Yellow Fever. I thought of the Black Vomit Yellow Fever Rico had died of. "*Vómito Negro*" was the Spanish term for the last stages of the disease, but only in certain cases. The disease wasn't as strong in Central and South America as it had once been, but it is quite strong today in areas of Southeast Asia. Like Vietnam and Laos. My antenna went up again. Something was wrong here. Wronger than wrong. I'd missed something significant. Okay, Rico was real sick. You don't get that sick without being sick for a while and knowing it, I mean there's treatment for Yellow Fever, and if you had it you'd damn well make sure you got help, saw a doctor, something. Today, with the right treatment you could almost be cured. Yeah, in times of stress, weakness, sickness, the chills and fever could come back. But nothing like Black Vomit. That was only in the last stage of an untreated case, most cases never got that extreme, never ended that horribly. That was what happened to an unvaccinated individual, one who was untreated for some reason. Neglected. Like if someone wasn't getting treatment because he was being held captive by someone. Or out of the country. I was beginning to get the picture.

Black Vomit. The more I thought of it the more the sick, twisted pieces began to fit together. Rico had not recently become infected, and for some reason he had not wanted to be treated—or could not get treated. Whatever the reason, it was too late by the time I saw him.

It was all bullshit. All fucked now. Rico must have told me a judicious mix of lies and truths, but I had no way of knowing what was a lie and what was true. What I thought had been truth...was it lies? What I thought had been lies...dare it be true? Who could tell? Not I. And Rico wasn't talking anymore.

But the big question was this. What was Rico doing with an untreated case of Yellow Fever in a low-life dive on the West

Side of Manhattan?

It didn't take me long to figure it all out. Or at least, what I thought it might be about. At least as much as I was capable of figuring out. I figured it had to do with one thing—the biggest, sweetest moneymaker of the last three decades. Now bigger and meaner and tastier than ever.

Drugs.

Drugs had to be the reason, the motivation moving the behind-the-scenes truth of what was going on. I smelled drugs everywhere I looked in this. It was an old and familiar scent to me, though I'd managed to be off the stuff for a few good years.

Yeah, it had to be about drugs, and that could explain why all kinds of weird crap was happening. And it was hot, with all kinds of people from the very lowest scum up to the very highest big-shots who didn't want the drug and cash gravy train to ever end.

Drug money was the sweetest of sweets.

It was free money.

I figured I knew it all now. The American MIA's were all dead, but there had been a handful of deserters who had also been listed in the group, listed as MIA but were still alive—now very active in the Southeast Asia drug trade. Oh, there couldn't be more than a dozen but they had to be the basis of all the MIA sightings over the years. And now they were the only ones left alive—the real MIA heroes were long dead.

It stunk.

* * * * * * *

The night was dark. Dreary. Raining like a bat outta hell. My run-down room creaking and groaning from high wind and hard rain pounding the outside of the building.

I never saw the big black Buddha that hit me. But he was there when I woke up and he had a gun on me, and a look on his face that said, I was a dead man for sure.

I was bound. Gagged. A desk lamp was tilted so the light

shone in my face. It was like the old third degree and I expected the rubber hose and the questions to be coming out any moment.

I was wrong.

Johnson undid the gag.

He put his finger to his lips and said, "Be very, very quiet."

I said, "I'll tell you whatever you want to know."

He smiled, said, "I don't want you to tell me anything, Mr. Powers. I just want you to die."

I knew there had to be something else.

There was.

He said, "But before you do, I want to tell you a story, Mr. Powers. It's something I've never told any other man. It's something I've wanted to speak about for over twenty years, but in the business I am in, it is impossible, forbidden to speak of such things...."

"But since I'm going to die anyway...."

"Precisely, Mr. Powers. And there's something else. You're a 'Nam vet, so you will understand and even might have a particular interest in what I have to say."

I gulped, wondering what craziness I was in for now, as my mind raced to find some way out of this, some means of escape.

I knew I had to keep him talking, so I told him, "All right, go ahead, you've got, like, a captive audience."

He liked that. Smiled. "Indeed I do, Mr. Powers. Indeed I do."

He grew real serious then. I thought he was going to pop me right then and there. He got up, began pacing the room. The flashes of lightning and pelting rain outside lent a deathlike eeriness to the scene. A desperateness I felt down to the bone. Even with the light off in my dive of a room, lightning flashes exploded constantly outside now, growing, with booming thunder, illuminating the darkness, sending rays of harsh light through my uncovered windows to play across the deep furrows of Buddha's big black twisted face.

"They were still alive, as late as 1980. I don't know how many exactly. Rico figured up to 500. Maybe, but I figured there was less. Had to be. No one knows for sure. I saw a couple in 1976. Dragged in chains along a path of the Ho Chi Minh Trail. In Laos."

"The MIA's," I whispered.

"Yes, the true heroes of the Vietnam War," Buddha said. His sweaty, big black shiny face had tears dripping down it now. "Oh, I was on the rolls, just like Rico was. MIA. But we weren't in the same league. Not fit to be listed with them. They were heroes. We were...deserters...and...."

"...and traitors." I finished.

"Yes. Some of us sold out. To the enemy. We went over to the other side. We were young. Scared. Stupid. No excuse. There weren't many, not many at all, but there were a few."

"And you?" I asked. I just wanted to hear him say it.

"Yes...." His whisper was so low it was almost lost in the tide of pelting rain and booming thunder. But I heard it. I would have heard it had the world exploded.

I sighed. "I guess it sorta figures."

"Haven't you ever done something you were sorry for, Mr. Powers? I mean, done something, something really terrible?"

I nodded. I had to say it. It had to come out. He was quiet. Waiting. I said, "I murdered an innocent women. It was years ago, but I...I had no right. I just killed her in cold blood because I didn't want to leave a witness."

"And it's been burning in you ever since, Mr. Powers?"

I nodded.

"Then you do know how I feel. I'm a loyal American, but I've been a traitor. I'm in the CIA, but then again, I guess that depends on which CIA, you mean, doesn't it?"

I looked up at Johnson then. I didn't see a terrible black Buddha anymore, just a rather terrified, and suddenly very old man sorry for all the bad things he'd done a long time ago. And the terrible things he was going to do in the future. Like kill me, probably any minute.

"What do you mean when you say it depends on which CIA?" I asked.

Johnson just smiled. He had that look, like he knew a lot of something that I didn't. And he wasn't saying.

The wind outside crashed against the building. Thunder boomed like an artillery shell, and the door burst open and a group of men dressed in black with M-16's flooded through the door and the windows.

Johnson drew his piece but he was blasted from a dozen weapons before he ever knew what hit him.

He was dead instantly.

I freaked. Shouted for help, for release, scared I was next. Johnson's blood had sprayed on my face. It was hot. It was dripping down my cheek. I shouted but no one seemed to hear me. A couple of the SWAT guys took out Johnson's body. Then they all left. Suddenly I was alone. Still tied up, but all alone. The thunder boomed louder, as if anger and rage from the very heavens, and the rain poured down in sheets. No one else in the hotel seemed to have heard anything, and the rain and thunder just shouted worse than ever. Growing mean.

Then I heard the footsteps out in the hallway. They were getting louder, coming closer. A man was approaching, and soon he came through the opening where the door to my dive of a room had been. A flash of lightning from outside lit up the room for a second. I saw who the man was. It sent a chill through me. It was Derrick Johnson. The white guy!

He came over to me. Bent down low so his lips were near my ear.

I sucked in breath. Fearful to release it. Looking into his stone cold eyes as they bore down into mine.

I was still tied up. I was helpless and at his mercy. He was the "other" CIA guy, maybe the "real" CIA guy? And yet he scared me more than Buddha did, and Buddha had admitted he was going to kill me. But somehow, I couldn't believe that. I figured it was Buddha's way to tell someone who knew how he felt the real truth. One of these guys worked for that "other" CIA? But which one? Buddha had admitted as much, that there were two CIA's.

"Rod Carew. You should have stuck to baseball."

I gulped and tried a half-assed smile that didn't work.

"Are you going to release me? Or kill me?"

He ignored that. He slowly withdrew something from his pocket. It was a knife! One of those Swiss Army-type, all-purpose knives, and he opened it up so that I could see the blade. A knife to cut my bonds? Or to cut my heart out with?

"Look, I don't know what you know. We don't know what you know. We don't care. As long as you keep it to yourself. Understand? The second you open your mouth about any of this you'll never talk again. *Comprende?* Do I have your full cooperation in this? It is a national security matter, Mr. Powers? Yes, I know your real name."

I nodded.

"That's not good enough. You must promise me, Mr. Powers. You have amnesia, you've forgotten about all of this; it's like it was erased from your mind. Do you understand? You'll never speak of it again. Do I have your solemn promise on that, Mr. Powers?"

I said, "Yes."

"Yes, what, Mr. Powers?"

"Yes, yes, I promise never to speak of it again!"

I flinched when he drew the blade down to my neck, but all he did was cut the rope there that bound me. Then he cut the rope on my wrists and ankles.

I shivered. I still couldn't move, my arms and legs were too numb from circulation loss. I just sat there. Open-mouthed. Trying to think. And not doing a very good job of it.

"And now you are free to go, Mr. Powers," Johnson said simply, as he refolded his Swiss Army knife and dropped it back into his pocket.

"And that's it! I'm free? Really? I make a promise and I'm free? What is this, the honor system?"

"It's your word, Mr. Powers. You make a promise and we expect you to keep it. Or else. Remember, this is a National Security matter. You publicize this and you will be silenced, discredited. In your case, that shouldn't be hard for us to do. It's a government thing. All you have to do is cooperate. Cooperate with your government, Mr. Powers. Be a loyal American...cooperate."

"Cooperate with what? A cover-up? Just like during the war. The crap never ends. Oh yeah, the war ended, but the bullshit just keeps rolling along."

"Mr. Powers, don't be difficult...."

"*Eat me!* I know what you want to do. You're no better than the damn NVA. Now you want to brush the MIA issue under the rug. I thought it was all about drugs, but it wasn't! It was so you and the people you represent can make a ton of blood money by opening trade and diplomatic relations with these fuckers. Like nothing ever happened! Like our guys just went on some fucking holiday! You know, those guys never came back. And they killed them all! Murdered them all, five years after the fucking war was over! All that don't seem to mean much to you."

"You are a fool, Mr. Powers." Johnson said, suddenly breaking into a terrible wracking cough. He quickly withdrew a clean white handkerchief, deftly putting it up to his mouth as he hacked a wad of phlegm into it.

Black vomit.

And I thought, good riddance, he was dying, just like Rico.

I said, "I think I've figured it. Damnit! I was such a fool. He was dealing drugs but he really was the good guy! He told me he wore a white hat and he was right. That fucking big black Buddha deserter bastard—he really was the good guy! And that makes you the bad guy, and now you people have won again."

Johnson just smiled and left. He was gone in a heartbeat.

* * * * * * *

I just sat there. The rain pelting down, the lightning flashing in anger all around me. And me wondering. Thinking about Rico. About black Buddha the traitor. Well, maybe he was, maybe he wasn't. About two CIA's that were at war with each other. Maybe at war with the country too? Thinking about 500 MIA's no one will ever see again, and a bunch of deep graves in the Laotian jungle no one will ever find. And the whole damn thing made me sick and I had to cry for a long time about it.

I cried about all of it. About all my brothers left behind. About the dirty murder. About the stinking cover-up. The worst form of betrayal. About greedy guys and corporate yuppies getting rich while a bunch of kids grew up without fathers, while wives went on without husbands, while parents never saw their sons again.

And I cried for a country that had been great once, but now just seemed as dead as all those MIA's who would never come home again.

realized I had never known what squalor meant.

One look at the shack my Lucy had grow up in, I knew why she ran away at fifteen.

It smelled something awful, and I could smell it a mile away: of cooked fish and chicken and stale watermelon and bad moonshine; of unwashed clothes and body and bad breath and dirty feet.

I heard a man yell: "GET YOUR SORRY BEHIND MOVING! YOU WORK FOR YOUR KEEP HERE, GIRL!"

Her father.

She had told me enough about him.

Sitting outside the shack was a skinny girl about ten or eleven in a dirty sack dress ripped on the side, showing a lot of pink leg. She was blonde and looked like a younger version of Lucy.

"Hello, Mister," she said.

"Hi. What's your name?"

"Ellie."

"Hi, Ellie. Is Lucy around?"

"Lucy? She sure is. Out back. Why?"

"I'd like to see her."

"Oh she's with child, you know," Ellie said.

"I know."

"She ain't as much fun as I can be." She smiled, showing me one missing tooth. She informed me for five dollars, she could please me with her mouth all night long.

"I need to see Lucy," I said.

"Suit yourself. Hey, what's your name?"

I told her.

"You're the baby's father," Ellie said.

"That's right," I told her, "and I've come to claim what is mine."

I found Lucy in the back of the shack, sitting in front of a washtub and cleaning a pair of men's long johns in the water. She was dirty and sweaty and her belly enormous. She looked like she was going to explode any second and a thousand little spiders would come flying out of her.

"Lucy," I said.

She froze, and turned.

"Jack?"

"It's me, baby."

She tried to get up and nearly fell backwards. I rushed toward her, grabbed her arm, stopped her from falling into the tub of dirty water.

We embraced.

"Oh Jack, what are you doing here?"

"What do you think?"

"How did you find me?" she asked.

"I asked around. I wasn't gonna give up."

"How did you know I'd be here?" she asked.

"Where else would you go."

And she asked: "Why did you come lookin'?"

"To have my family back," I told her.

She cried and I tried not to cry.

"I was so scared when all that stuff about you was in the paper, and people were talking. I didn't want them talking about me and I didn't want to be in no paper, so I ran. I ran back home."

"I know," I said.

"I'm so sorry, Jack! I was scared witless!"

"Hush," I told her, "it's okay."

"And they said you had a wife...."

"I'm not married to anyone but you," I said—a lie, but I would get to the truth later. Now wasn't the time.

A large man in his fifties burst out of the back of the shack. He wore dirty blue boxers and an old t-shirt with dozens of holes. He had a cigar in his mouth and held a jug of moonshine in one hand.

His other hand was missing. I vaguely recalled Lucy telling me her father had lost part of his arm in a mechanical accident of some sort.

"Lucy!" he bellowed. "Who's this fellow?"

Ah, the backwoods and all its colorful glory.

"Daddy, why it's Jack, the one I tol' you 'bout."

He sneered and looked me over. "You the one who got my Lucy in the family way?"

"Yes, I did, sir," I said.

"And I suppose you come here to make an honest woman of her?"

"I came here for her, yes, and for our baby."

"Well, too bad," he said. "Too late. Look at her. She was once the hottest piece of chicken in these hills and caught quite a price. Think I can sell that blimp? And she won't be good for trade until at least two months after she pops that rugrat in her belly. Your rugrat. Come back for the rat in a month, you can have that, I don't need to feed that mouth, but Lucy stays. She shoulda never ran away in the first place. You bet I gave her a good beating about it, baby or not. Shoulda beat that brat right out of her. Did it to her no-good tramp ma a few times, best thing I ever did."

He took a puff and then a drink.

We stared at each other.

"Well, boy, git," he said, "this is my land, what I say is law."

"No, sir," I replied, "I'm taking Lucy with me."

"The hell you is, mister. This here is my land and I own everythin' on it, including that pair of milky tits and string legs you got your arms around. Now, you got five bucks, you can have some fun time with fat Lucy there, but I got another girl, real young, who can do you better for ten."

I hated the bastard.

"No, sir," I said, "Lucy and I are leaving."

"Lucy?" he said to her.

She looked down. "He's the father of my baby," she said.

Daddy stomped toward me and got into my face, waving that lit cigar in front of my nose

"You git, boy, if you know what's good. I buried half a dozen bodies out back, and no one ain't ever gonna know or find them. Make you number seven, I will."

I slugged him one.

Right in the nose.

Same punch I had given Jed, back when we were laying pipe and when he was taking nude photos of my wife.

A good punch that breaks noses and makes blood flow.

Daddy grunted, stumbled back, and fell flat on his wide rear. He stared at nothing, like he couldn't believe what I had done.

"You can't do that," he said.

"I just did."

"This ain't right."

"You treating Lucy that way ain't right," I said.

"My land, my property, I am the law," he said.

I kicked him in the belly and he doubled over, vomiting moonshine and something pink he had been eating.

"Not right," he mumbled.

Lucy hugged me.

"I somehow knew you'd always come and rescue me," she said. "My knight...."

She packed what few things she had and hobbled out of the shack. I told her I had a car half a mile away. I didn't want to drive up and give her daddy warning.

Ellie watched us and asked, "Where you two goin'?"

"Far away," I said.

"Take me with you," she said.

Lucy's heart broke, I could tell.

"I can't leave her here with him so he can keep sellin' her body," Lucy said.

"Okay," I said.

* * * * * * *

We live a quiet life, the four of us, my family. The baby was born two weeks after I pulled Lucy out of the grip of her father. The baby was a boy and we named him Roger.

I got a job in a tanning factory. It pays decent, sixty dollars a week. It keeps a roof over our heads and food in our mouths.

She has another baby coming. She wanted this second one.

When she was five months, she told Ellie that it was a sister's duty to keep the man of the house happy when the wife was unable to.

Did I object? I'm a man, I have needs. So young Ellie started to share my bed, and now she's three months pregnant.

There will be three babies in this little place we rent. We'll have to find a bigger home, and I'll have to get a second job.

I've stopped writing stories. That was just a hobby.

Roger is out of prison and writing romance novels under a female pen name.

Some nights I share the bed with the sisters, one on each side of me, both plump from my seed.

In a way, it is Biblical.

It's the way the world is.

BLACKMAIL BABE

We were playing weekly bridge with Sam and Patty McPherson. They lived across the street. My wife, Elaine, mentioned our issue with finding a good babysitter for our two sons, ages five and three. "We've gone though *four* the past year," Elaine said; "they're all flakes."

"They never show up on time," I said.

"One never showed up *at all*," Elaine said. "We still don't know what happened to her. Probably eloped or...who knows."

"We missed the first act of this wonderful play," I said.

"We'd been planning that night out for *two* months!" Elaine said.

"Oh, you should hire our babysitter then," Patty McPherson said. "She's wonderful, absolutely wonderful—always on time, doesn't raid the fridge or smoke pot in the bathroom, and the kids just love her." She added: "And doesn't bring boyfriends over for some illicit flesh time."

I noticed Sam's face twitch.

"Is she truly reliable?" I asked.

"She is," Patty said.

"I must have her number then," Elaine said.

"Just don't book her when *we* need her," Patty said

"She could pull double-duty, going back and forth, crossing the street," I said.

"What's this girl's name?" Elaine asked.

"Sandra Boise," Patty said.

At the end of the night, Sam leaned over to me and said,

softly, "Be careful."

"What?"

"You'll know what I mean," he said.

I guess he meant this Sandra Boise and her allure, her body, her hair. The girl was a knock-out, that's for sure, and she knew it. She was five-foot-seven, perhaps a hundred and ten pounds, a Eurasian with smooth light brownish skin and green eyes. Her blonde hair was a dye-job and suited her well, with a strand dyed purple. Her mini-skirt was so short that I hoped she was wearing panties in case she shifted or bent over—then again, another part of me, the dirty married man part of me, hoped she wasn't wearing panties, and I might get a glimpse of some forbidden fruit. Her breasts were small and that was usual for girls with Asian blood; her halter was so tight that the fabric outlined her nipples.

I opened the door when she rang the bell. She licked her eighteen-year-old lips and said, "Mr. Challon? I'm Sandra Boise, the babysitter."

"Yes, yes," I said, unprepared for such a sight.

"Is that the babysitter, dear?" Elaine said from upstairs.

"Yes," I said.

"Tell her to come on up."

"The kids are upstairs, already in bed," I told Sandra Boise.

"Cool," she said. Walking past me, my nostrils were treated to a mixture of her perfume and something else—that indescribable scent of teenage girl. Yes, I know what Sam meant. Or did I?

I was distracted when I drove. Patty and I were going to see a film at the art house, one of those complicated European movies.

"What do you think of the babysitter?" Elaine asked.

I was thinking about what she looked like naked. "What?" I said. "Oh, she seems okay."

"Okay? Did you *see* that skirt?"

"Skirt?"

"Don't you play coy," said my wife, "I know *very well* you noticed."

"It was...something," I said.

"How do girls get away with skirts so short today? It should be a crime."

"A crime," I said, "yes."

"Hello? Are you on earth?"

"Yes."

"Where's your head?"

Up Sandra Boise's skirt. "Some work issues," I said. "The new test drug...."

"Right," she said. "Well, I guess short skirts and all legs, um, that's the style today. What will be the style when our children are in their teens?"

"Total nudity," I said, "see-through clothes."

"Don't doubt it."

The art film was long and boring and there were a lot of naked men and women in it. Every time I saw a naked female form on the screen, I thought of the babysitter. This was horrible. I was a married man, nearly forty. I looked at other women, sure, but I never gave so much thought to actually doing something.

I was nervous about going home and seeing Sandra Boise and her skirt and legs again. I was nervous about smelling her again, but of course I was looking forward to the guilty pleasure of it.

She was watching television and eating a green apple when Elaine and I arrive home at 11:30 p.m.

"How was the movie?" she asked.

"Bah," said Elaine. "How were the kids?"

"Quiet and asleep."

Elaine went to check on the kids. Sandra stood up, smoothed her skirt, but I did catch a glimpse of her yellow panties and I had a feeling she wanted me to.

She reached into her backpack and pulled out an apple and offered it to me.

I laughed at the symbolic absurdity.

"Something funny?"

"Only to old men who read too much," I said.

"You're *not* so old," she said coyly, with a coy smile.

Reached for my wallet and paid her: $20 an hour. She took the bills and carefully placed them in her sock. It was a show: a show of legs, of ankle, of feet...of skin.

"I saw that movie you went to see," she said. "I liked the sex scenes."

"There seemed to be a few," I said.

"Well," she said, "I better get going."

"Going?"

"Home."

"I'll drive you home."

"Oh thanks, but no thanks."

"I have to drive you home."

"*Have* to? Is that protocol?"

"Well...you don't have a car, right?"

"There's the bus," she said.

"Bus? Nonsense."

"There's an 11:45 and a 12:15 down the street, leaves La Jolla and goes downtown, I take it all the time."

"At this hour?"

"Sure."

"It can't be safe," I said.

"It's safe," she said, and she said, softly, "I know how to take care of myself, Mr. Challon, I'm not a little girl, you know."

"I insist," I said.

"I insist on taking the bus," she said. She looked at her watch. "And I better go now if I wanna catch the 11:45. Thanks, Mr. Challon, and I hope to babysit for you again!"

Just like that, she was out of the house fast, and I couldn't help myself but watch her rear end bounce, and the subtle way the skirt flapped so again I caught a glimpse of panties.

Elaine walked down the stairs and yawned and said, "Where's Sandra?"

"She left."

"She what? Aren't you driving her home?"

"No."

"She have a boyfriend pick her up or something?"

"No, she's taking the bus."

"*The bus?* Where does she live?"

"Downtown somewhere."

"Downtown? *That's crazy!* David, go get her and drive her home. A girl her age and dressed like that doesn't take a *midnight bus* all the way downtown by herself."

I wanted to say, "She can take care of herself, she's not a little girl." I left the house, got into the car, and drove down to the bus stop around the corner. The bus was leaving. I saw Sandra's head by a window. She wore headphones and was nodding her head to music. There was only a few people on the bus.

I couldn't go back home and face Elaine. Decided to follow the bus. It didn't make many stops at this hour, going down La Jolla Boulevard, merging into Pacific Beach Boulevard, then getting on the freeway straight to downtown San Diego.

Downtown was alive—the clubs, the restaurants, the young people drinking and dancing, the out-of-town men with call girls on their arms. Sandra Boise got off at Fifth and Broadway and walked down to C Street, to a loft building. Kept my distance, watched her enter the building. Well, at least I could tell Elaine the girl got home safe. And I knew where she lived. Or did I? Maybe she was visiting a boyfriend.

Elaine was asleep when I got home half an hour later. Slipped into bed, spooned my wife, and thought of Sandra Boise's miniskirt and legs.

* * * * * * *

Over the next two months, we hired Sandra Boise three times. Each time, she wore something enticing: tight jeans with rips, tight black pants, another miniskirt. Each time I offered to drive her home, she refused. I went out to the car so Elaine would think I took her home. The second time I told Elaine a boy picked her up. The third time, I drove to the bus stop. She was sitting there, headphones on, legs crossed, in that damn mini-skirt. She pulled the headphones off and said, "Mr. Challon?"

"Get in."

"Mr. Challon, I don't think I should."

"Get in, damn you," I said.

She stood up and got into the car.

"Don't drive yet," she said.

"I'm taking you home."

"That wouldn't be a good idea," she said.

"Why not?"

"Why do you *think*?"

"You afraid I'll rape you?"

"That might be fun," she said, and giggled.

"What the hell," I said.

"*Don't* drive," she said. "What do you want? Do you want to cheat on your wife? Do you want some young ass? Is that it?"

"I, um," I didn't know how to answer that.

"Look, look here," she said. She arched her rear up, pulling her mini-skirt back. She pulled off her panties. They were thongs. She was completely shaved and smooth. She touched herself, patted herself. "Is this what you want?" she said, opening herself with two fingers. "Mr. Challon, this what you want?"

"David."

"Huh?"

"Call me David."

"*David,*" she said softly, "is this sweet little pussy what you want?"

"Yes," I said, reaching for it.

She slapped my hand away. "And what if I give it to you? What about your wife? She'll smell my fuck on you. She'll wonder why you were gone so long. She'll divorce. Is this pussy worth losing it all?"

"Please," I said.

"Not tonight," she said. "You come see me tomorrow afternoon, say, 1:30 on the dot. You come see me and you can have this kitty." She gave me her address, but I knew it. I didn't have her loft number.

"My bus is coming," she said, getting out of the car.

She left her panties on the passenger seat.

"Bring them to me tomorrow," she said. "Tonight, do what you want with them. But bring them back, David."

She got on the bus *sans* panties. I watched her get on the bus and it was obvious she wasn't wearing underwear. I was delirious with lust; enchanted by this young vixen. I snatched the panties and placed them to my face, inhaling: the smell of her perfume, her skin, her pussy. Jesus Christ, I was dizzy.

* * * * * * *

I had trouble sleeping. I had stashed the panties in the garage. I kept getting out of bed to go to the panties, to smell them, to touch the delicate, feminine fabric and image what it would be like to hold the girl, to kiss her, to make love to her.

At the office, I kept the panties in my desk drawer and took them out every half hour. I couldn't get any work done. I told my boss I was taking the rest of the day off after lunch, that I had some personal things to take care of.

"I hope everything is all right," my boss said.

"Fine, fine, just—nothing major."

I worked near downtown, so it wasn't a long drive. I parked in a bank lot that was three blocks from Sandra's loft building. I walked. The panties were in my jacket pocket. I kept my hand in the pocket, fondling the object I was here to return.

I went into the loft building, took the stairs to the second floor. #2-D she told me. She didn't live with her parents, not in a loft; I wondered how a girl her age could afford a place like this. Lofts were not cheap down here, at least $2,000-3,000 a month. Did she have roommates? A boyfriend? Just before I knocked, I wondered if she were setting me up, that some thug was going to answer the door and beat the crap out of me. "You like little babysitters, eh, pervert?" he'd say, smashing my teeth in.

Sandra Boise answered. She was wearing jeans shorts and a

yellow baby doll shirt. "You're right on time," she said. "Come on in, David."

I stepped inside. The loft was small: a futon bed in the corner, two small couches, a TV. Clothes were scattered on the floor. There was a kitchen area and a bathroom.

"You live here alone?"

"Why do you ask?"

"Just wondering...."

"What?"

"Babysitting pays well," I said.

"I keep busy," she said, "like you—you have something for me?"

"Oh yes," and I took the panties out of my jacket pocket, handed them to her.

"I bet you had fun with these, hm?"

I shrugged.

She tossed them to the floor, with other panties bras, mini-skirts, jeans, halters—all the necessary items of a sexy teenage minx.

"Want something to drink, Davey boy?"

"What do you have?"

"Beer, soda. Milk, water, beer."

"Beer, sure."

She went to the fridge in the kitchenette, took out two beer cans, opened them. I watched her ass sway in the jeans, watched her bend as she opened the fridge. I couldn't take it anymore. I went to her. I spun her around. Grabbed her. Held her. Tried to kiss her.

"Hey," she said.

"You invited me over."

"So fast."

"Going out of my mind."

"Have a beer, man," she said, "and chill."

Drank some beer but didn't let her go. My hands roamed her body: her neck, her breasts, her stomach. She didn't stop me. She drank beer. We drank beer and kissed. She spit beer in my mouth. Removed her baby doll shirt. No bra. Kissed her breasts, brown nipples erect.

We kissed and groped and undressed from the kitchenette to the futon. We were naked. I explored her body with my mouth and she did the same. "Just so you know," she said, "I swallow." I couldn't wait. She didn't ask that I wear a condom and I didn't think of bringing one. When was the last time I had used such an object? Back in college?

We made love in several positions: she was on top, I was on top, doggy style, she on her stomach.

I was about to reach the proverbial orgasm and spill myself into the girl and that is when I heard the clapping of two hands and a male voice: "Bravo, dude. Good show. One of the best."

I moved away from Sandra. She laughed. "Not bad," she said.

A tall, skinny man, in his mid-twenties, emerged from the bathroom. He was holding a tiny Sony camcorder, the kind with the flip-out screen. He moved in close.

"I should have waited for the finale," he said, "but, you know, I don't like other men coming inside my wife. Makes me feel—icky later on."

"Sorry, David," Sandra said.

Was trying to process this. "What the fuck" is all that came out of my surprised and stupid mouth.

"Here's the deal, Mr. Challon," the guy said. "My name is Scott, and I'm married to Sandy here. I've been watching and recording the whole sordid thing—you coming here, a man old enough to be her father, seducing her, drinking, kissing, doing the nasty. What would happen if a copy of this tape was delivered to your wife? To your kids, for god's sake? To your co-workers? How much damage would that do to your life, buddy?"

I started to get dressed. Sandra remained on the futon, naked, smiling. The tall guy kept recording.

"Turn that off," I said.

"Sure," he said. "I have the evidence."

"This is some kind of joke?"

"No."

"What is it?" I asked Sandra.

"Blackmail," she said with a shrug.

"You have money, live in La Jolla, have a good job at a pharmaceutical company."

"Money?" I said. "This is about *money*?"

"Money makes the world go round," Sandra Boise said.

"You two want cash," I said. Laughed. Laughed loud, shaking the head. "You're nuts," I said. I went to the fridge and got myself a beer. "You're clowns, the both of you."

Was a show: wanted to appear cool, tough. I was scared.

Drank.

Beer.

I said, low, "Money."

"Look at this dude," the husband said. "I like him. He's not like the others."

"No, he isn't," she said. "He knows how to screw."

"I'll be going now," I said.

"Ah-ah," the tall skinny husband said. "Moo-la-la-la. Unless you want your wife to find out about this."

"Do you want to go through a divorce, David?" Sandra said. "Lose the house, the kids, half your money...your life."

"How much?" I said.

"Twenty grand."

I laughed.

"We know you got it," Sandra said.

"What makes you think I can just get you twenty thousand?" I said.

"Educated guess," Scott said. "But we're agreeable to an installment plan. Say, a thousand a month for twenty months, or two thousand every month. Or you can pay a grand for half a year, then a lump sum. Either way, it comes out to twenty."

"Why?"

"A girl has expenses," she said

"So does the husband," Scott said. "I'm eager to be a filmmaker, see, and Sandy wants to act, and we have this loft, and, well." He smiled.

"Why me?"

"You wanted my pretty little shaved cunny," she said.

"The wages of sin," Scott said.

I played scenes in my head: Elaine getting the tape, a copy getting to my boss. The arguments, the shock, the lawyers. The kids. The shame. Moving. For what? For some eighteen-year-old Eurasian slut in a mini-skirt?

"I know what you're thinking, David," Sandra said. "I know what names you're calling me in your mind."

"Keep them to yourself," Scott said. "That's my wife."

"You little twerps," I said. "Okay. You got me. Twenty thou. Fuck me."

"I did," Sandra said.

"I'll give you two grand now," I said. "I can do, say, a thousand a month, maybe two for a while, and my wife won't notice. I'll try to get a balloon payment together in the meantime."

"Sounds good," Scott said.

"Do you want a check? I have fifty bucks on me."

"The check is in the mail and I won't come in your mouth," Scott said. "Here," and he handed me a slip of paper with numbers on it. "Wiring instructions: router, account. Wire the two k today, and then the first of next month, another two k, or one, whatever, one or two, but no less, or else your wife gets a surprise from the FedEx guy."

"Once the twenty is paid, then what," I said.

"You get the master copy." Scott held up the camera.

"How do I know you won't keep copies? You won't keep squeezing me for more money?"

"You don't."

"You just have to trust us," Sandra said.

"Funny," I said, finishing the beer.

"You have no other choice," she said.

No, I didn't. I left them, and went straight to the bank to complete the wire.

* * * * * * *

This went on for three months. I paid two grand the next month, one the second, two the third. Sandra kept babysitting for us. I couldn't tell Elaine that I wanted to fire the girl; she was the best babysitter we had and I had no good reason that wouldn't raise suspicion. Every time Sandra came over, wearing something sexy, we exchanged secret glances: the sins we shared. I drove her home, too. One time, she had me stop the car and she climbed into my lap and we had sex. I couldn't resist, and I figured why not, I was paying for it. "You're evil," I said. "You love me," she said.

Jesus, *did* I love the girl? Why couldn't I keep my hands off her? Driving home, I thought if only Sam and Patty McPherson hadn't recommended her. And Sam had warned me, too. Warned. Oh, hell, *I wasn't the only one.* Why did it take me so long to figure this out?

The next day was Sunday. I walked across the street. Sam McPherson was watering his lawn.

"Hey, Dave, how are things?"

"Swell, Sam," I said. "How about you?"

"Oh, can't complain."

"Really? No stressful situations, no heavy bills?"

"Excuse me?"

"You still using Sandra Boise to babysit?"

He was nervous now. "Yeah. Good kid."

"Good pussy, too, eh?"

"Say what? David, how can you...?" He looked at me. "Crap."

"You warned me."

"What happened?"

"How much you paying her and Scott, monthly?"

"Fifteen hundred."

"And they have you on tape with her?"

"You too?" he said.

"Are there more of us?"

"Steve Ryan."

"Steve?" I said. The Ryans lived five houses down.

"Steve's wife recommended Sandra," Sam said.

"How many other suckers are there? How much are those grifters pulling in a month? We need to go to the cops."

"Hell no," Sam said. "Patty would...no. Too much to lose."

"You ever been out to the Anza Borrego dessert, Sam? About ninety miles northeast from here. Big and vast, there are places humans haven't tread ground for hundreds of years."

"Say what?"

"I have an idea," I said. "Let's go talk to Steve."

We walked down to Steve's house. His wife said he was in his study, working on the western novel he'd been writing the last four years. Steve was in his late forties and an antique gun fanatic: he had rifles and old pistols mounted on his wall. Two years ago, he had taken me to a shooting range with him.

"Listen to my proposition, Steve," I said, "and then never, ever bring this up again."

* * * * * * *

Sam's wife and kids went out of state to visit her mother the next weekend. Sam called Sandra and told her he had come up with the balloon payment. "You can come and get it," he said on the phone, "but come alone. Don't bring the hubby. This will be it."

"You just want one final poke," she said. "Well, you earned it. I'll be there in a couple hours."

She took the bus. She wore black pants that were like paint on her body, and a purple sweater. It was getting cold out.

"Sammy baby," she said, kissing him, walking in. She didn't expect to see Steve Ryan and myself waiting.

"A party," she said.

Steve pointed an old Remington six-shooter at her. It was on his wall, not having seen action in more than a hundred years.

"Oh, man," she said, and laughed.

"This is serious, Sandy," I said.

She stopped laughing. "Oh, shit."

The four of us drove downtown to pay a visit to her husband.

We used Sam's mini-van. Then we drove out to the desert.

The three of us were very quiet when we drove back from the desert that night.

For a long time I waited for the police to come. After three years, I figured we were in the clear. Steve Ryan and his wife moved to Wyoming after his big western novel was published and made into a movie. Sam and Patty McPherson divorced after she was caught having an affair with some professor at the university and they both moved.

Five years later, I saw it on the news: the mummified remains of a man and woman in their twenties found out in Anza-Borrego State Park. "Police are saying it appears to be a murder-suicide," said the pretty blonde news anchor on the TV set.

I PAID THE WHORE

I.

"This has to stop," I said.

"It'll never stop," she said.

I slid the envelope across the small table in the bar. She opened it, looked inside, counted the twenty-five crisp $20 bills straight from the ATM machine.

"Five hundred, just like I said," she said with a nod and a grin. "If you're anything, you *are* reliable."

"If I'm anything, I'm a sucker," I said.

She downed the rest of her rye and ginger ale and waved to the bartender for another.

What the hell, I'd have another beer. I felt like getting drunk— any man who was being blackmailed would want to get drunk.

"Cynthia," I said, "this is going to stop."

"That may be your wish," she replied, "but your wish won't be granted."

The bartender brought over another rye and ginger ale and bottle of beer. I paid him, with a two-dollar tip. He gave me a sly wink.

II.

Same bartender, always the same guy, the same wink, the same drink. No, not the same—I was drinking vodka tonics that night, two months ago, when I met Cynthia here. I'd been having some troubles at home and at the job and I just wanted to drink my night away to oblivion; I wasn't looking to get laid. There was Cynthia, all dolled up in a tight-mini skirt and her hair in pig tails like some naughty nymph school girl, although she was pushing the wrong side of twenty-five.

I woke up in her studio apartment, a few blocks from the bar; woke up with one hell of a hangover. I didn't remember having sex with her but we must have because I was naked and there were the telltale sighs of dried fluids in my crotch.

"You were great last night, David," she said.

"How do you know my name?"

I never tell a one-nighter my name, not my real name.

"While you were asleep, I looked through your wallet," she said.

Wench! I pulled my wallet out. Money was in it, but I had no idea how much I'd spent last night.

"Don't worry, *David,* I didn't rob you."

It wasn't my money I was worried about—it was my driver's license, with my address, and my business card, that told anyone I worked at the D.A.'s office as a junior prosecutor. And there was a dry cleaner's receipt with my home phone number on it.

"Come back to bed," she said, but I got out of there.

I lied to my wife, Betty; said I had crashed under my desk, working on discovery for a major case. She believed me because it's something I actually did now and then, and she liked it, she thought I was being ambitious, to move up in my career.

Cynthia called my house thee days later. I expected it at some point. I deal with criminals all day at the office.

"Meet me at the same bar," she said.

"No," I said, my voice low, "I'm not interested in a repeat performance."

"If you don't, I'll keep calling back and your wife will wonder. And I'll call when you're at work...at the District Attorney's."

"I'll be there in a few."

"I'll be waiting, David."

"We're out of milk," I told Betty.

"It can wait," she said.

"I have a craving," I said.

"You know what the doctor said about your triglycerides!"

The bar was a ten-minute drive into town. Cynthia was at the same table, like she lived there.

"Buy me a drink," she said.

I waved at the winking bartender.

"What do you want?" I asked.

"A drink."

"You want more than that."

"Right to the point," she said.

"Don't have all night."

"$5,000."

"You're crazy."

"I know you have it," she said. "I saw one of your ATM receipts. You have $13,537.32 in your account."

"That money belongs to my family."

"A wife and two kids, a son and a boy. I saw the photo."

"You looked at everything in my wallet."

She sipped her drink and smiled.

"You bitch," I said.

"I won't deny it."

"You expect to blackmail a prosecutor and get away with it? Extortion is a Class B felony, lady, and it'll get you two-to-seven."

"And *what* will it do to your reputation as a prosecutor if it got out that you slept with someone who is not your wife?"

"Everyone makes mistakes."

"And that someone has an arrest record for prostitution and drug dealing."

She had me there.

"And what about your family? What would Betty say? The kids? The in-laws? Would Betty stay with you if she knew you'd skewered a hooker?"

She had me there as well.

"A thousand," I said.

"Five," she said/

"No."

"Or else," she said, smiling, sipping.

"I'll deny it."

"I have a Polaroid and some nice photos of you knocked out, nude, and drooling on my bed. It's cute."

"How can I believe you?"

She shrugged. "Do you wanna risk it?"

Yeah, she had me all right.

III.

So I paid the whore.

But blackmail never ends. Three weeks later she called me at the office and I met her on a park bench outside city hall.

She was dressed well, had gotten her hair dyed from blonde to red.

"I need more money."

"I gave you five," I said. "You blew it all that fast?"

She said, "Money doesn't last. I got a car, and I got a better apartment, a nicer place really, and clothes, and that tapped me out, you know."

"No," I said.

"Here," she said.

She handed me an envelope. There were photos in it, all of me. She was in some of them, naked, holding the camera up. In one, she had my penis in her hand.

"What do you need?"

"A grand," she said. "You can afford that."

"You have no shame," I told her.

She said, "I'm just a girl trying to survive, David."

IV.

You'd think I could do something, being a prosecutor—talk to my boss, the D.A., so this could be handled gently and indiscreetly. That was fantasy—there'd be a grand jury, the press would get wind of it, and then my wife.

So here I was, back at the bar, my third payment, this time five hundred. I knew it wouldn't be the last; she'd call again once she went through the cash.

I felt something just awful so I got drunk.

We both got drunk. I mean, she was there.

"Let's go somewhere and have fun," Cynthia suggested.

"The hell with you," I said. "That one time cost me enough."

"No charge."

"Said the whore to the lawyer."

"You'll like my new apartment," she said.

"I'm going home."

I stood up. I was quite drunk, but I could drive home. It was only ten minutes away.

Cynthia was drunker and she could barely walk. I helped her outside. It was raining. The roads were shiny and slick.

"You better take a cab," I told her.

"That costs money."

"I'll pay."

"No cab! I have a car!"

She stumbled to a beat-up 1972 Camero.

This is what she spent my money on?

"Don't drive," I told her "You're too sauced. You'll hurt someone—and yourself."

"The hell with you!"

I wouldn't let her get in the driver's seat.

"How far away are you?" I asked.

"A mile or two."

Against my better judgment, I decided to drive her home. I could take a cab back here, or to my house. I was still a defender of the law, and I'd seen too many innocent people hurt and killed by drunk drivers.

The rain came down harder. I drove slowly. Cynthia kept telling me to put my foot down on the pedal. She giggled and grabbed my leg and pressed down on it. The Camero speed forward. I saw something jump out into the street—a cat, a dog, a possum, something—and I swerved to avoid it.

Lost control of the car. Spun out.

Crashed into a telephone pole.

IV.

Don't know how long I blacked out. I woke up in pain and Cynthia was halfway out the window, her body a bloody mess, her neck cut from the glass. Her eyes were open. She was not alive.

She hadn't put her damn seat belt on.

I stepped away from the wreck. Her car was pretty much wrapped around the pole. How the hell did I survive this?

It was quiet, except for the rain and distant thunder.

I had to get away from this scene.

Walked back to the bar and flagged a taxi.

V.

Betty was in bed, back home, and reading a book. She smiled at me. I smiled back. I took a shower and got into bed.

She was in the mood.

I wasn't.

"Hard day at work?" she asked.

"It was no picnic," I said.

I got into the mood, though.

I was feeling better—one of my troubles was erased.

SUNLIGHT REFLECTIONS
ON A CRUSHED BEER CAN

1.

She watches him again. Bobbi Sox Thorn stands at the window and commandeers these cheap binoculars she stole from WalMart two months ago. She eyeballs the guy in the trailer across the yonder way. She spies for movement; seeks proof he's there. Yeah, she could go outside, and stroll by, ear wax his TV on Fox News, hear him doing *clack clack clackity-clak* on his typewriter. Every time she does this, he stops *clack clack clackity-clacking*, the TV turns down, and then he stands by the window of his Airstream trailer. He stands there and eyeballs her, like he *knows* she's watching him. Bobbi Sox finds this embarrassing and she always runs away. She's no stalker, just curious. She finds herself drawn to the neighbor and his *clack clack clackity-clack*. Bobbi Sox Thorn watches from the window of the double-wide trailer she shares with her husband, Johnny Ray Thorn, binoculars in palm and at eyelash.

Let's face it: Bobbi Sox's bored as crusty cheese on a stale cracker and needs some excitement. Nothing ever happens in this fucking boring trailer park. She's fifteen and married to a man three times her size and twice her age (or so Johnny Ray claims to be: thirty-three) and who has a brain three times smaller than her squishy stuff. Her husband ain't the brightest used light bulb in the room, but *she* at least has some smarts: subscribes to the *Reader's Digest*, reads the tabloids in the supermarket, knows there's a world out there somewhere. She knows the guy in the Airstream is from *that* world; she has heard that he comes from California. What he's doing out here in Hannah, Alabama, living in a nowhere trailer park, is beyond anyone's noggin. What is he doing, *clack-clack-clackity-clacking* away on a typewriter machine device thing? Doesn't he have a computer? Even Bobbi Sox has a laptop—Johnny Ray stole her one off a truck in the city a couple months ago.

Bobbi Sox thinks he might be on the run from the law; he's hiding out, having killed someone or embezzled money or whooped ass on his girlfriend so hard that he put her in a coma and knocked out all her teeth. Just thinking about that slapping around gets her panties knotted up, even if she isn't wearing panties right now. She likes it when Johnny Ray slaps her a few times when she pushes him away before pumping her pussy. She's feeling horny but doesn't want to wake her husband up for a romp and stomp; she'd rather go over to the Airstream and do the sexy hop with the typewriter man.

She knows this much: his first name is "Bill." He looks to be in his late thirties-early forties: tall and thin and wears glasses and has shaggy, curly brown hair. Bobbi Sox wants to suck his cocks. She wants to lick his balls and then kiss him so he can taste his own salty ball cheese, the way her stepdaddy used to like. Thinking all this dirty stuff makes her eyeball her husband and think about waking him up with a blowjob. Problem is, Johnny Ray, being so big, has a cock so huge and thick she can barely get her mouth around it, but he does have enormous balls and he hardly showers so they always smell real funky the same way her stepdaddy's balls used to stink. And that's just nice.

Johnny Ray: see him there asleep on the couch, in front of the TV. On the TV: a re-run of *Family Guy*, an episode Bobbi Sox has seen three times, where the Griffin clan relocates to a small Texas town because people believe Stewie is possessed by Satan. Around Johnny Ray: six crushed beer cans. Pabst Blue Ribbon, of course—what else would a big ol' trailer park hillbilly drink? All she has to do is eyeball at him for a long minute and any sexual feelings she has goes away like a possum running underneath the floorboards: Johnny Ray is six-foot-six, 380-pounds, balding with a dirty blonde mullet; half his teeth are missing; he has zits all over his neck and shoulders; he snores and farts when he sleeps; he drinks all day, he never has a regular job. Well, it's not like they're always poor—Johnny Ray makes money from selling drugs, selling stolen shit, and beating up people who owe the local loan shark. He steals shit too, like she does.

She goes back to the binoculars.

She thinks her husband's asleep; she thinks Johnny Ray hasn't a notion of what she's up to. But Johnny Ray knows. Her back turned to him, he opens an eye and looks at her ass in those cut-off denim shorts she always wears, the ones where her left ass cheek always hangs out. He thinks she is casing that guy's trailer out—the new guy from California. He thinks she is planning a good robbery for them both. He has no idea that his wife wants to fuck the guy from California.

2.

In the local grocery store, Bobbi Sox Thorn is slapped across the face with shock and awe, or just something crazy: she's looking at one of the tabloids about Hollywood movie and TV star and she thinks she sees a picture of *him*, Bill, her neighbor who goes *clack clack clackity-clack* all day on a typer machine.

But *it is* him....

...a picture of him with this TV star on his arm, this woman who plays a nurse on a show Bobbi Sox has seen a few times. Under the picture is a caption: "Five months after divorcing LeAnn Raines, A-Lister script scribe William Reynolds has been missing in action. Could he be penning his next series or a feature?"

This is crazy! thinks Bobbi Sox.

"This is crazy," Bobbi Sox says out loud.

"What's crazy?" the girl at the checkout stand says, and then goes, "Hey, you gonna buy that zine or what?"

"Yeah, yeah," Bobbi Sox says. She hands over the tabloid.

And she sees him again:

He's at the other counter, buying milk and cheese and beer.

Bill. William Reynolds.

He sees her seeing him and he quickly looks away.

This is no coincidence, she thinks.

"None at all," she says.

"Huh?" the girl at the counter says.

"Nothin'," Bobbi Sox says.

Says the girl at the counter, "You should stop talkin' to yourself all the time, Bobbi Sox Thorn."

"Shut up and minds your own bees-wax," says Bobbi Sox.

"I'm just sayin'...."

"Say nothin'."

"Whatever," says the girl behind the counter. "That'll be $9.89 total."

Bobbi Sox hands over a ten-dollar bill. *Bill!*

William Reynolds—Bill!—quickly leaves the store.

This all means something and Bobbi Sox decides she's gonna find out. It feels like destiny. Why else would she both his photo and his own self at the store at the same time? The Universe is telling her something.

"The Universe is tellin' me somethin'," she peeps out loud.

"It's tellin' you, 'eleven cents change'," goes the girl behind the counter, handing Bobbi Sox a dime and a penny.

3.

That night, Johnny Ray slaps her around when she says, "No," and then pump-fucks her four times in three hours. Even with that weight on top of her, all Bobbi Sox thinks about is Bill Reynolds. She imagines the neighbor pump fucking her and this makes her come ten times in a row. This pleases Johnny

Ray to no end. "See," says her huge husband, "see how much you really like it? How come you always fightin' me about it? Or do you just like me knockin' your brains around in that li'l skull?"

4.

She's gonna get to the bottom of this destiny shit one way or the other. Bobbi Sox has a plan. She sees Bill Reynolds leave in his car, an old Volvo something, and anticipates his return: she wears the tightest cut-off shorts she has, and a see-thru white halter top. She does outside and waits. She does some jumping jacks to get the sweat going, so that her tits stick to the halter and her nipples are more obvious. Oh, she knows what she's doing, she knows what a naughty little trailer park vixen she is, this Bobbi Sox Thorn.

Bill returns. He ganders her. He tries to ignore her. That ain't gonna happen, she's gonna catch him, she's gotta! She bends down, ass out his way, acting like she's tying her shoe or something. Her ass cheeks stick out and the crotch of the shorts rides deep into the crotch of Bobbi Sox. She's not wearing panties again, she can feel the air and sun on her quim; she hopes some pussy hair is sticking out so Bill can get a nifty scope.

He's holding two grocery bags.

"Oh, hi," she goes.

"Afternoon," he goes.

"Watcha got there?"

"What?"

"It's so hot and bothered today," she says, pulling at her halter. "You don't happen to have some soda pop, or maybe a beer in those bags there in your strong manly arms?"

"Um."

"Sure you do."

"Yeah." Sheepish smile. "Yes, I do."

Bobbi Sox: *I gotcha, Bill Reynolds.*

"Could you do a thirsty girl a favor an offer me a soda pop?" she says. "Or even a nice cold ice cold beer?"

"Um," he goes, "sure."

Bobbi Sox: *Yep, gotcha.*

5.

Inside his Airstream, inside his lair, his cave, his abode: Bobbi Sox glances around. So this is how the other half lives. Impressed, envious, how sparkly clean and neat everything is, unlike her run-down trailer and its smells of rotting food, stale beer, and ass. And the trash everywhere, and the skid marks on the toilet. *She wants to live here!* She has never known a man so clean. She wonders if he's a ho-mo-sex-y'all. No, not the way he is checking her out: he is straight like any George Washington, who fathered the country: she catches him checking out her nipples.

He asks, "So what would you like, a soda or a beer?"

Says Bobbi Sox, "Dunno," and she goes, "How 'bout both?"

"Both?"

"Double-fisted," she says, holding up both hands.

"Okay, sure," he says. He pulls out six packs of Diet Pepsi and Budweiser from the bags, putting them in the fridge, removing one of each.

The girl looks around more: on a fold-out table sees an Olympia manual typewriter with a sheet of paper in it; next to the typewriter are two stacks of paper: blank and written on, double-spaced.

He opens both the soda and beer and hands them to her.

"Thanks," she says.

"No problem."

She runs the cold beer across her face, and then her chest. "That's the ticket."

"It's warm out."

"Hot."

"Yeah."

He gets a soda for himself and opens it.

Says Bobbi Sox, "What's with this typewriter thing?"

"I'm writing something."

"I hear you."

"Um?"

"I hear you *clackity-clacking* on this machine."

"I'm sorry—does it bother you?"

"Not at all. Just wonderin'."

"Wondering?"

"What you're writin'."

"Oh," he says, "a novel."

"Oh," she says, "so you're a writer?"

"Yeah."

"Any your books famous?"

"Haven't published a book yet. I mostly write movies, screenplays."

"In Hollywood?"

"That's where...I live," he says, drinking his soda.

"Any movies I might know?"

"I don't know if they play out here. Ever seen *Beverly Hills Gun Down*?"

"No."

"*Funny Money Men*?"

"No."

"*How to Win a Diamond Ring*?"

"I don't get to the movie house much," Bobbi Sox says, "and we only get three channels on the boob tube...."

"We...?"

"...husband and me."

"Oh, yes."

"You seen him around?"

Bill makes a face. "Yes."

"He's a...." She slugs down the beer. "That's the ticket."

"Want another?"

"How can a girl go no?"

She touches the manual typewriter the way she might touch a large penis, and this of course is all intentional and for Bill's sorry gaze.

"Why don't you have one of them laptops?" she asks. "I got one. But I don't know how to use it much."

"Wanted to write my novel the classic way, the way writers used to long ago," he says and hands her another beer.

"What's your novel about?"

"Life in a trailer park."

"Really?!" She perks up. "This one?"

"No, the one I grew up in."

"Grew up?"

"It's a coming-of-age novel, set in a California trailer park."

She steps around the table and stands close to him. "You wanna know what life is like in a trailer park?"

"Um," he says, nervous: her breasts touch his chest, he doesn't know what to do. Bobbi Sox knows she has to make the first move so she grabs Bill hard and kisses him.

"Wait," he goes, "what about your husband?"

"Fuck my husband."

Says Bill, "No thanks, I'd rather...."

"What?"

"I'd."

"Say it."

"...rather fuck you."

"How could a girl go no?"

6.

Doing it with Bill: so much better than Johnny Ray. Bobbi Sox has never been with a man who is gentle, who touches her face and kisses her nose and says how pretty she is. Come to think of it, she's never been with *anyone* except Johnny Ray— he did after all pop her cherry and married her and there's never been anyone else except for those boys she would kiss and give blow jobs to when she was eleven, and there was her stepdaddy, but he never fucked her, he just had her to lick the sweat off his balls like all little girls do with their little tongues. None of that was really *sex* or...making love.

Says Bill, "What if your husband knows?" he says this a couple times as they spend a couple hours fucking a couple times and she says, "Don't you worry none, he sleeps all day and wouldn't notice a Woody Mammoth walkin' by."

"You mean Woolly Mammoth."

"Eh?"

"Not woody."

"Hey, I just got wood on my noggin," she goes, grabbing his dick, "and I see you got wood too."

Says Bill, "Oh boy."

Says Bobbi Sox, "Bobbi Sox loves dem cocks."

Trudat.

7.

She returns home and sees her dear husband laying on the couch, snoring away, his enormous white, hairy belly moving up and down like slow elevator on the fritz.

8.

Bill ganders Bobbi Sox as she leaves, eyeballs her ass swaying this way and that way; remembers touching that ass, kissing that ass, *fucking that ass*, the best piece of young ass he's ever had in his life—better ass than any Hollywood starlet—and he says to himself: "Are you *crazy*, Bill? What the *hell* are you doing, doing that sexy young *thing*?" How old is she? He's afraid to ask. He thinks eighteen or nineteen. No, he doesn't know she's fifteen, doesn't know she can fib her age the way Traci Lords hoodwinked the pornographers in the 1980s.

He didn't come here to *fuck* trailer park trash; he came here to *write* about them. He came here for *isolation.* He came here to get *away* from Hollywood. He came here to *get away* from his ex-wife and ex-girlfriends and any other woman he got entangled with, and here he is getting entangled with another married woman. "Do you ever learn from past errors, Bill Reynolds?" he says to his reflection in the mirror. "Remember the *last* married woman you fucked?" That married woman—the wife of a studio head—destroyed a movie he was working on and sent three bikers to cripple him. He wasn't home when the bikers arrived, but a friend of his was, this friend who needed a place to stay, this friend who was now in a wheelchair in place of him. That was the kicker: that's when he knew he had to get the hell out of Los Angeles and go somewhere remote, a trailer park in the middle of nowhere in Alabama, and finally write that auto-biographical novel he'd been threatening to write over the past decade in La La Land.

9.

He tries to write that night but all he can think of is Bobbi Sox and her ass and pussy and hard flat stomach and he can't write so he drinks, and drinks.

10.

Bobbi Sox thinks of Bill as Johnny Ray pump fucks her; she thinks of how Bill touched her and kissed her and how Johnny Ray never kisses her, just pump-fucks her, does his things, rolls off, burps, farts, and goes to sleep. How bahhhh-ring. Yawn. Zzzzzzzzzzzzzzzzzzzzzzzzz....

11.

Bill tells himself it won't happen again but it does happen again: Bobbi Sox comes over in the afternoon, wearing another skimpy outfit, something that's a makeshift schoolgirl's outfit, and he can't help himself. "Gotta soda pop for me, Mister?" she says and he goes, "I have something else for you to put in that mouth" and she says, "Oh, what, pray tell, can that be, Mister?" Oh no no no—he cannot pry himself from this velvety vixen and they go at it for a couple hours and then she leaves and all night he thinks about her visit the next day, hoping for it to come soon, hoping it won't happen, but it *does* happen. It happens *every day* that week, and the next. It becomes a *routine*.

It'll end soon. He's only thirty pages from completing the second draft of his novel. Should take two weeks tops, then he'll quietly slip out of the trailer park, go west, back home, wayward angel, and forget all about Bobbi Sox and her great devilish blowjobs.

12.

Bobbi Sox dreams of moving to Los Angeles with Bill and becoming a TV star. Or a porn star. Either is fine. Better than *here*.

13.

At first, Johnny Ray Thorn has no eye-dee-er what his sexy young wife is up to as he sleeps the day away. He may be a big mindless brute, but he ain't no dummy. Soon enough he figures something is up. It's the way she is when he pumps her: usually she gets into it, she comes a lot, now it's like she's somewhere else, *thinking of someone else*. And there was the time she was gone when he woke up, and when she came back she was surprised he was awake.

He asked, "Where ya been, Bobbi Sox?"

She went, "Oh, out and about."

She was like, "Takin' a stroll."

She said, "Nowheres special."

He smelled something and it smelled funny. "You smell like beer."

"What?" she said, cocking her right hip a certain way that always drove him crazy. *"What,"* she said, "can't a girl have a beer on a hot day?"

"Ain't so hot."

"You know I *like* my beer."

He smelled something and it smelled funny. "You stink like fucking."

"Just my juicy pussy," she said, "it's been *all wet* and wantin' to wrap herself round your *big fat cock.* You know how Bobbi Sox *loves you cocks....*"

14.

Bobby Ray Thorn is gonna get to the bottom of this. He's gonna find out what Bobbi Sox is doing when she steps out of the trailer thinking he's snoozing. He's faking it: snoring and everything, one eye barely slit open, watching her watching him. She wears a skimpy little cotton dress that clings to her body nice-like; he can see the outline of her thong panties. This cannot be good, and Johnny Ray's fears and suspicion come true: he spies out the window and witnesses Bobbi Sox knock on the door of the trailer across yonder, where that fella from California lives. He knows nothing about the guy, doesn't even know the guy's name. He sees the guy, though, he sees the guy open the door of his Airstream and Bobbi Sox goes inside with a bounce to her walk that Johnny Ray knows well: it's the way she bounces when her pussy is wet and bothered.

Rage rushes through Johnny Ray's blood like a crazy herd of rabid bobcats. He takes in a deep breath, the way he's seen Buddhists do on TV. He slugs down half a fifth of Teacher's to ease his nerves. Maybe there's a good explanation for what he saw.

Nope.

He goes over to the Airstream, doesn't knock, walks in, and this is what he sees:

Bobbi Sox sucking the man's cock.

The man's naked and lying on the bed and Bobbi Sox's naked. The two are in the 69 position. Johnny Ray cannot eyeball the other man licking his wife's poon, but he sure can gander his wife eating that peckerwood.

Bobbi Sox looks up and sees her giant husband and, cock in mouth, she screams.

The scream is muffled, of course.

It's the last sound she ever makes in her young life.

15.

It all happens so fast that it amazes Johnny Ray Thorn how easy, how quickly, a person can die, just out of the blue.

The California guy and Bobbi Sox jump up from the bed, stark nekkid. At first Johnny Ray eyeballs the guy's tubesteak and wonders why Bobbi Sox would want *that* when he's three times bigger. *Whatthefuckever.* The man and Bobbi Sox look for a way out of the Airstream but there is no way out, and Johnny Ray grabs them both by the hair and smashes their skulls together.

Splat, squish, end of the song, baby girl.

So quick, so fast, so easy!

Holy splatter mania!

The two skulls cave in on impact and their eyes pop out like cartoons and blood and weird yellow gooey matters comes out of their ears.

"Bobbi Sox?"

But she's dead.

And the guy's dead.

Johnny Ray sits down on the bed.

He smashed his wife's head.

He looks at the man instead.

All he could see was red.

He was so angry, his blood was like lead.

"Shit."

He lies down on the bed and closes his eyes until he stops seeing red.

He sleeps some.

He thinks.

He sleeps some.

He thinks.

The bodies smell: they have both shit and pissed themselves. He's seen what happens to people when they die. They start to go stiff and ripe. Seven hours have gone by and Johnny Ray didn't even know it. Seemed like seven minutes.

"Shit."

16.

It's dark out. Johnny Ray has a shovel. He digs a deep hole. He drinks a whole fifth of Teacher's as he does so. He opens another fifth. It's the last Teacher's he's got. Damn, that hole is deep. It's deep and big enough for two bodies. He rolls the two stiff smelly bodies into the hole. He covers them with dirt. Pack it in, make it look right. *Looks good.* You can't tell a hole's been dug unless you gander real hard. He pours some motor oil over it all. He says a little prayer for his wife's cheating soul. "You had it comin'," he says to her damned soul, "you shouldn't't've gone and done that. There's only one cock you suck, cocksucker: *mine.*"

17.

Inside the Airstream. Johnny Ray wipes off anything he may have touched. This guy's trailer is too damn clean for his own good, like a queer's. But the guy was no queer, just a fella who liked to steal other men's wives and had death coming to him the way a fella has a stack of buttermilk pancakes coming when walking into an I-Hop. He notices a stack of papers by a type-writer on a table. Stacked like pancakes. Looks like the guy was writing something. Johnny Ray eyeballs this:

SUNLIGHT RELFECTIONS ON A CRUSHED BEER CAN
by
William Reynolds

The fella was some kind of writer of some kind, eh.

18.

The next night, sober, Johnny Ray drives the Airstream a mile away from the park and leaves it on the side of the road. He takes the typewriter and the manuscript pages with him. He walks the mile back home. He stops off at the gas station and buys a twelve-pack of Pabst Blue Ribbon.

19.

Johnny Ray takes the 500-odd pages of the manuscript back to his trailer and reads some of it. He's not a good reader, he's a slow reader, and he likes the story. It's about a young boy growing up in a trailer park and his daddy is a mean drunk and his momma is a drunk and a whore and the young boy gets *say-dooced* by a twenty-year-old woman in the park who pops his cheery and sets him on the grand road to manhood.

It's not unlike Johnny Ray's life.

Kinda similar.

He had a daddy like that and a momma like that, but no older woman ever popped his cheery. Johnny Ray popped his cheery when he and some buddies all gang-banged this thirteen-year-old on meth. Johnny Ray fucked the girl five times over the course of twenty-four hours. Boy, that was the times, when a guy was young and innocent and not married to a slut, a slut like his momma used to be. Johnny Ray now knew why his daddy hit his momma so much.

He reads and reads and drinks the twelve-pack, and then sleeps some and when he sleeps he thinks.

20.

He's gotta get out of here.

No one will be asking around for Bobbi Sox, they have no friends or anyone who cares. But people might ask about this William Reynolds, and the cops will wonder why the Airstream was left abandoned by the side of the road.

Johnny Ray takes out the money he keeps behind the toilet that Bobbi Sox never knew about. Emergency cash. Any smart man has a stash. $750.

He calls his cousin in Tallahassee, Florida, and says he needs a place to lay low. "My wife done and left me, cuz," he says.

Says cuz, "Come on over then."

Johnny Ray takes the Greyhound out to Florida. He brings the typewriter and manuscript. He reads the rest of *Sunlight Reflections on a Crushed Beer Can* during the ride. He wishes there was more sex in it. The narrator muses on someone named Derrida too much. And someone named Mark Twain. But it's a good story.

21.

He stays a few with his ol' cousin and his cousin's wife, a sweet little thing but not so pretty, not like Bobbi Sox.

"It sucks she left you," says cousin.

Says cousin's wife, "It's horrible."

Says cousin, "Stay as long as you need."

The wife, one day, sees the manuscript pages and goes, "What's that there?"

"Oh," says Johnny Ray, "somethin' I wrote."

Why did he say that? Why did he lie? It just came out of his big mouth.

"Really?" says cousin's wife. "With that typer?"

"Yep."

"Didn't know you're a *writer*."

"Yep."

"*Hot damn*, a writer in the family."

"Yep."

"Can I read it?"

"Yep."

But before he gives her the pages, he types out a new title page:

SUNLIGHT REFLECTUNS ON A CRUSHED BEER CAN
by
Johnny Ray Thorn

It takes him nearly twenty-five minutes to type that out, since he's never used one of these machines, and he doesn't notice he misspelled "reflections."

22.

Cousin's wife reads it and goes, "My God, *you're smart.* You sure can write. Are you gonna get this published?"

"Dunno," says Johnny Ray.

"You *should.*"

"Guess so."

"You *gotta.*"

"Dunno how. How does someone get published?"

"You send it to a publisher," cousin says.

"Where you find them?"

"Dunno," says cousin.

"*Yellow Pages* maybe," says cousin's wife.

"They're in New York I think," says cousin.

23.

One day, cousin's wife comes home all excited and says she has info for Johnny Ray. She says she went to the library and asked the librarian how a body would get a book published if that body wrote a book. The librarian said, "First you need to get an agent." The librarian then handed cousin's wife a big book called *Writer's Market.*

Cousin's wife ripped out the pages with "literary agents" and ran out of the library.

"Here ya go," she goes, handing Johnny Ray Thorn the torn pages.

There are dozens of names and addresses. Johnny Ray's confused. He says, "Which one should I send it to?"

Cousin's wife closes her eyes and lands a finger on one of the pages and goes, "That one!"

24.

Johnny Ray Thorn goes to the post office and sticks the 503 pages of the manuscript into a big padded envelope and mails it to an agent in New York City. Cost for mailing: $12.40.

25.

"You has a letter!" cousin's wife says three weeks later.

It's a letter from the agent's address, but not from the agent. It's from an "assistant." Some fella named George. George writes: *I read your novel and love it. Please call me, you didn't leave a phone number.*

Johnny Ray calls the number. George seems excited to talk to him. "I can't make a decision of repping you," says George, "but I've given it to my boss with a shining report and two thumbs up."

"Does that mean you'll publish it?" Johnny Ray asks.

"Oh, not us," says George, "but we'll find someone to do that, hopefully."

That night, Johnny Ray and cousin and cousin's wife celebrate by drinking a bottle of Teacher's and some beer.

26.

That night, cousin's wife comes to Johnny Ray where he's sleeping on the couch and she's plum buck nekkid and goes, "I'm so horny right now. I ain't never fucked anyone who's gonna be famous. You're gonna be a famous author soon and I wanna say I fucked someone famous once."

He's tempted but: "No, I can't do that to my cuz, or to any man's wife."

She understands.

"You're so noble," she says.

Says she, "That Bobbi Sox is a fool for leavin' you."

Says Johnny Ray, "Yeah."

27.

A week later, the agent calls Johnny Ray and says he read the novel, his assistant raved about it, and he wants to "represent" Johnny Ray.

"What does that mean?" asks Johnny Ray.

"It means I'm your pimp and I'm going to sell your southern genius ass."

28.

Three weeks later, the agent calls: "I have five major houses in a bidding war."

"What does that mean?"

"It means you're going to get a big fat advance check."
"A what?"

29.

Three days later, the agent calls: "The highest bid we got is six hundred thousand."
"Dollars?"
"Cash American."
"Oh, my."
"What do you say?"
"Say?"
"Wanna say yes?"
Johnny Ray says, "Yes."

30.

Details come, contracts signed, check arrives a month later from the agent, minus 15%. Johnny Ray is rich the way Rabbit was once rich. He gives a few thousand to his cousin for letting him crash on the couch. He buys a Mustang Camaro (1973, rebuilt) and drives back to Alabama and rents a nice big house with three rooms. Does he need three rooms? He likes having three. He buys one of those wide-screen plasma TVs. He gets cable and 150 channels. He has hookers come over. He drinks prime whiskey. "Thank you kindly, Mr. William Reynolds," he says every night, like a prayer.

31.

Thirteen months later, Johnny Ray flies to New York City for a party at some art galley, celebrating the birth of *Sunlight Reflections on a Crushed Beer Can*. He sticks out because everyone wears suits and evening gowns and smells nice and Johnny Ray wears overalls and an old white T-shirt and boots and stinks like mildew. The New York people find this "cool-io" and "hipster hick," and they think he's wearing a costume like the characters in the book. Everyone in New York publishing is small and pale, and Johnny Ray towers over them all. A woman in a mink coat wants to fuck him. A man dressed as a woman wants to fuck him. A waitress in a tux serving drinks wants to fuck him. Johnny Ray's amazed with shock and awe-shucks: all for this book, people want to fuck him and give him money and tell him what an *artiste* he is. "The new Faulkner," the critics say. He has no eye-deer-er who Faulkner is. "The child of Flannery O'Connor and Truman Capote," is what one newspaper review goes. The agent tells him all the reviews coming in are positive. Johnny Ray has no desire to read them, if he could read them and understand what they're gabbing about, postmodern this and post-structural that, "avant-pop" and "hipster hick." He gets drunk instead and looks at all these people like he's watching some circus show. It's entertaining for sure.

32.

He takes the woman in the mink coat back to his hotel room at a place called the SoHo Grand, where drinks cost forty dollars each. He wonders if he should have picked the tranny, he's always been curious about chicks with dicks and what that might be like. The mink coat lady, who's about thirty-five-years-old and has fake breasts, cries after he fucks her, and goes, "You're so big, I've never been filled like that." She cries more and goes, "I married a man worth twenty million and I'm miserable, it makes no sense." She leaves him her cell number and leaves his room and takes a taxi cab home. If he had known she was married, he would've picked the tranny or the waitress. Live and learn in the big city, Johnny Ray Thorn.

33.

Morning. The agent calls and tells Johnny Ray Hollywood wants to option *Sunlight Reflections on a Crushed Beer Can* for half a million dollars and five percent net.

"What do you think?" the agents asks.

"What does this mean?"

"Means they'll make your words into a film and you'll get another big fat paycheck. What do you think of them green apples, huh?"

"Lotta apples."

"How you felling about this? Tell me now."

"Funny how things happen," says Johnny Ray.

Says the agent, "Ain't it, though?"

THE AGENT

1.

Okay—so you're at this party in Tribeca and you really don't want to be here, but...here you are. What you hate about the evening: very little, if any, business calls. You keep checking your cell to make sure it's getting reception. You strike up a conversation with a young woman with long brown hair; you really like her eyes. She touches you, you touch her back; you play with her long hair, twist it in your fingers, smell her perfume and tell her you approve of the scent. The next thing you know you're in one of the bedrooms having sex with her on a pile of coats. When this hasty act is done, you leave the room first. No one at the party seems to notice your indiscretion; you stop feeling guilty and begin to feel like the conqueror—like a Norseman who has just ravaged some princess on the high seas of a badly written Viking romance novel. You get yourself a new drink, and you *need* a drink; you go out to the balcony and sit down. Two minutes later, the young woman joins you. She also has a cocktail, and she appears freshly fucked—glowing and smiling.

"So," you say.

"So," she says.

"That was something else," you say.

"Oh yeah," she says. "Do you do this sort of thing often?"

"No," you lie.

"Me either," she says.

You ask her name.

She says, "Trinity."

"That's really your name?"

"Like *The Matrix* movies," she says.

You nod and say, "I like it."

"That's my chat room handle anyway," she says. "Do you do the Internet?"

"Only e-mail."

"And porn?"

You smile and say, "Who doesn't look at porn on the Net?"

"My husband, he looks at it all the time."

"Your husband?"

"Jacks-off to the weirdest sites."

"Husband."

"You know my husband, right? I saw you talking to him like you were old friends. William Blount."

"Holy shit," you say, "you're Bill Blount's *wife*?"

"Relax," Trinity says. "He has no idea what we just did. He never notices anything. Terrorists could fly a plane into the building down the street and he wouldn't take heed. It's *okay*."

"I didn't know you were married."

"I didn't tell you," she says, and: "Does it matter?"

You're like, "No."

"Ever do cybersex?" she asks.

"Once or twice."

"I do it all the time," she says. "It's fun. I like it."

"Good for you."

"So what do you do? And what's your name?"

You tell her your name, and tell her what you do for a living.

She says, "An agent? Like, you represent *actors*?"

"Writers."

"What?"

"Novels and screenplays," you say. Under thirty, you're the youngest and hottest mover of product at a big and well-known agency; you know how to find the stars in the piles of manuscripts. You tell Trinity this.

"Oh," she says.

"Your husband publishes writers," you say.

"Oh," Trinity says, "I never talk to him about his work. Have you always been an agent?"

"I used to deliver pizzas when I was a kid," you say. "I was a bike messenger in college. Then I tried my hand as a junior stockbroker."

"Stocks!" Trinity goes. "I love playing the stocks. I have an Ameritrade account," she says.

"Yeah?"

"I," she says proudly, "am a daytrader."

You tell her you do a little daytrading on your Schwab account.

"Sometimes I make money, sometimes I don't," she says. "Usually I do. What I like most," and her eyes get this little *something* in it, "daytrading and having cybersex at the same time."

"Sounds like fun."

"So why aren't you on Wall Street anymore?"

"Stress," you say.

"There's no stress being an agent?"

"It's a different kind."

"As long as you're happy. Are you happy?"

You have to think about that. You say, "Yes." You say, "Yes, I am."

"That's good," she says, "it's good to be happy. That's all that matters, right?"

"Right."

She says, "So, who are your hot clients?"

"Right now I have two." You're more than happy to talk about this. "They're different as different can be. One is this wild fellow from Arkansas; he wrote a novel called *Sunlight Reflections on a Crushed Beer Can*. It's the ultimate tome on white trailer park trash. It's an unbearably sad work of bone-crushing genius—a 980-page monster of a book."

Trinity says, "980 pages?!" She goes, "I'll wait for the movie."

"There very well may be a movie," you tell her; "I'm talking to several producers. Now, my *other* precocity," you go, "has written a collection of eight stories, a slim but dynamic volume, called *Sex, Drugs, General Mayhem and Death in Junior High*. The writer, by the way, is a thirteen-year-old girl."

"Junior high is the worst," Trinity says, "kids can be truly evil in those trying and awkward years."

"Yes, that's what my young author claims."

"Uh-oh," Trinity says, "William is looking at us."

"He is?"

"It's okay. I better go to him."

"Okay."

"It was fun."

"Yeah."

She leaves. You stand there on the balcony. Your cell rings. The caller sounds far away—and he is. He's a publisher you know in Osaka.

"Takayuki-san," you say. "How goes it?"

"Let us talk dinero," Takayuki says.

He wants to buy the Japanese rights to four books you rep. You're ready to make a deal tonight; doing so makes you feel complete when you finally go to bed. You'll wake up feeling *right*.

2.

The next day—noon—interior: at the office—you get a phone call from Los Angeles (it's nine A.M. there, the day's just starting); it's Bernard Goldman, a producer, and he's distraught.

"Your client, man," Bernard says, "your client, Johnny Ray Thorn—"

"What about him?"

"—thought it was all an act, a ruse, you didn't tell me he was an *actual fucking hick*!"

"He wrote a novel about hicks," you say. "What did you

think?"

"But, yeah," Bernard says, "I didn't know he *was* one!"

"What happened?"

"I invited him to this party in Bel Air. Belairbelairbelair, and who do I allow to enter the gates of the Elysian hills? I guess I should have checked him out first, but man oh man you could've given me some kind of heads up here, guy. He comes to the fucking party in smelly old overalls and no shoes! All three hundred and twenty-five pounds of him! And he proceeds to get drunk as a skunk and grab-asses every starlet in the vicinity. Mind you, some of these girls didn't mind, they found him kind of amusing, but to me it was as embarrassing as walking into green light meeting without my prize Rolex. I mean, really, guy! I mean, I love *Sunlight Reflections on a Crushed Beer Can* and I want to get the abridged version up on the celluloid, but I'll tell you *this*—I do *not* want this hillbilly mofo on the set. I mean, he's talking like he'll be there, like he's going to be at every shoot and have say-so on all the dailies, but I declare this here and now, dude: it ain't gonna happen. No way, no how. He is not L.A. material."

"Bernard," you say sincerely, "I don't know what to tell you; I'm sorry the meet didn't go well."

"The guy can tell a story on paper, but he should be locked away for the good of all humanity."

"Nevertheless," you say, "the movie's going to be a hit."

"Let's hope so. After all, I'm *banking* on it."

"So let's sign on it."

"I can't yet. You know how it goes."

You always know how it goes.

An hour later, Johnny Ray Thorn calls from his hotel room in Century City.

"This place is weird," he says, "and the people are weird."

"Maybe it's time to go home, Johnny Ray. Arkansas is calling. Eh?"

"Arkansas can kiss my hairy ass," says Johnny Ray. "I booked a flight to New York. I'm leaving in two hours."

"New York?" you say, rubbing your forehead very hard. "Why New York?"

"Maybe I can do some book signings. I talked to the lady in publicity. She says she can set something up in a day or two. My novel is still selling, right?"

"Flying off the shelves," you say. "Flying."

"So no problem. I'm flying too."

"Well," you say, "call me when you get in."

"Isn't that little girl in New York?" Johnny Ray asks. "You represent her? The schoolgirl slut?"

You hesitate and then say, "Molli Runes. She is here doing promo stuff."

"Yeah, that's what I read. I'd like to meet her."

"She's very busy, you know."

"I wanna meet her."

3.

Molli Runes is at the SoHo Grand in a $600-a-day room. She has a reading and signing to do at six, another reading at nine, and two talk shows in the morning. Her story collection is #5 on The List, she's going to be in *The Village Voice*'s "Writers on the Verge" Issue, and you hear rumors she may be up for a PEN/ Hemingway Award. Or was that the Faulkner? You can never get the two straight—and does it matter? Either way, it's sales and attention and you've been telling her to get to work on that novel; and like any teenage girl, she's stubborn to listen.

You go to see her at the SoHo, to escort her to the readings/ signings; you are *not* prepared for this: a naked and apparently young author bouncing up and down on the bed.

She has a crack pipe in one hand, a lighter in the other. Her hair is sticking out in all directions. Her body is pale pink, her pubic hair wispy and her breasts like tiny apples (so they say).

"Hey!" she goes. "There you are!"

"Oh hell," you mutter. "Molli," you say, "please put some

clothes on."

You look at the wall.

She goes, "I know you're not such a *prude*."

You're like, "Get dressed."

"What do you have against the human body?" She hops off the bed and she's next to you, looking up at your closed eyes. She smells like hotel soap and rock cocaine. "Oh," she says.

"Molli."

She says, "Will you look at me?"

You look at her.

"Why don't you get naked," she says.

"Why don't you get dressed."

"Why don't we *fuck*," she says. "I need to get royally fucked. I've been smoking this bad shit for an hour and I'm horny as a horny toad."

She giggles.

You are *not* Humbert Humbert; still, you cannot help yourself from checking out her nymphet form. You fear she will destroy many men when she's ten years older, if she hasn't destroyed a number of men already. In her short fiction, the "I" has slept with teachers and older men who live across the street and give the "I" marijuana and tequila.

"Where," you ask, "is your mother?"

"She's not here."

"Where did she go?"

"She didn't *come*," Molli says. "She's back at home, fucking her new boyfriend."

"She let you travel *alone*?" you say, incredulously.

"I'm a big girl," Molli says, and then looks at her breasts. "Well," she goes, "maybe I'm *not* big," and giggles, "but I can travel to The Big Ol' Apple by myself. They gave me this room. I have my own credit card, thanks to you."

"Yeah?"

"Thanks to *you,* I'm semi-rich."

"Yes, Molli," you say, "and with such things—there is a certain amount of responsibility."

"Poo on that," she goes, "let's celebrate my impending fame." She tugs at your arm and says, "Let's have a sticky quickie." She says, "Don't worry, I'll never let a biographer in on this special moment."

All you can do is envision the repercussions. You're reminded of the James Bond movie *For Your Eyes Only*, and the scene where a blonde underage nympho ice skater tries to entice Roger Moore into bed with her pink naked body; but Bond says, "Don't grow up too fast," and turns her down. When you saw the movie, you thought: *Oh, Mr. Bond!*

You take Molli's crack pipe away.

She goes, *"Hey."*

You say, "There's a book to promote."

She goes, "Bummer."

You say, "This is your career."

She's like, "You have a point. It's all that matters, right?"

"Right."

4.

Molli does the Catholic schoolgirl thing: plaid skirt, white blouse, black penny loafers, off-white knee-high socks. This, you find, is more sexy than nudity. She knows what she's doing and you know she'll get far in this business, and for whatever duration (another collection, a novel, maybe a movie, then oblivion) you will get fifteen percent.

So, at the six o'clock bookstore gig, she performs well. She reads two stories from her book, thirty minutes total, and you're amazed at her delivery: the projection, the dramatic pauses, the levels in her voice, the various voices she gives to her characters. She must have had some training in drama or speech in her hometown, Seattle. There are about thirty people at the store and everyone buys books. A young man from the publisher's publicity department is there, and he says he has a limo to whisk Molli to her next gig.

"A *limo*," Molli says. "Coolness."

The limo has a fully stocked bar. Molli makes herself a vodka tonic; you know it's pointless to admonish her. You make yourself a Tom Collins, drink it fast, and make another.

"Better watch it," Molli says, "you'll get drunk."

"I never get drunk," you say, and this is true. You can drink and drink, and the best you can do is a damn fine buzz. You have never been shit-faced in your life.

"My whole family—alcoholics," she says. "Especially my Mom. Sometimes I think I *shouldn't* drink."

"You should not. You're too young."

She laughs and says in a snotty high-pitched tone, "And I'm too young to have published a book full of sex and debauchery."

She has a point.

She gives you her vodka tonic. "You finish it. I have another reading to do."

You drink her drink.

At the second reading, the one person you don't expect to see is there—you're hoping you wouldn't see him, not right now. Johnny Ray Thorn, all six-foot-five, three hundred-plus pounds of him. He's an impressive sight: barrel-chest, big belly, thick arms. His legs are very skinny. His hair is unkempt, unwashed, and he's missing several front teeth. What did the L.A. *Times* say about his author photo? *The most unattractive and scary-looking Southern writer since Harry Crews.* That's Johnny Ray Thorn, all right, and damn it all if you're not proud of the sonofabitch; you're just not prepared for him being here, *here*. At least he's wearing shoes. He's wearing the overalls; he's told you it's the only clothes he feels comfortable in. There are fifty, sixty people at this reading, and every one of them looks at Johnny Ray with the appropriate literary snobbish glance, one you've seen all to often, as if to say, "What is that trash doing here?" But a young fellow wearing a brown sports coat and horn-rimmed glasses says, "Aren't you John Thorn? You wrote that trailer park novel that's a bestseller, right?"

"Yeah," Johnny Ray says flatly, "that be me."

"I loved your book."

"Thank you kindly."

"Johnny," you say. "Jonathan."

"I love it when you call me that."

"You made it."

"It was a hairy flight," he says. "Hairy like a skunk's ass, and just as smelly. Lots of bumps in the air. What do they call that stuff? Turby. But I had this." He removes a flask from his overalls. "Always helps."

"And what's that?" Molli says, joining in.

"Moonshine, baby," says Johnny Ray. "Distilled it myself. My grandpapppy's original recipe."

"Wow."

"You're Miss Runes," says Johnny Ray.

"And you're Mr. Thorn," says Molli.

"Seems we have much in common."

"Yeah, our names pop up on the same bestseller lists."

"And we have this crazy man." Johnny Ray wraps a big arm around your neck. You wince. You smile. You can smell his armpit and it ain't a field of daisies.

Molli slaps you on the ass.

They both laugh.

"Well," you say.

"I read your stories," Johnny Ray says, letting you go and stepping toward Molli, looking down at her, "and I wanted to meet you."

Molli stares up at him like she would view a mountain in the desert. "I can't say I've read yours. I have it, but it's just too big for a girl like me."

"One day you'll be able to take it."

"I'm sure I will."

"Enough of this," you say. "Let's get out of here."

"Yeah," Molli says, "we have a stretch."

5.

There are five of you in the limo—the fellow in the brown jacket and a skinny clerk from the bookstore were invited by Molli and Johnny Ray; they are both aspiring writers and they want to show you their stuff, they want book deals, they want to be famous without having put in the work it takes. They are as common as nineteen-year-old porn actresses who've done one or two videos and have visions of money and underground fame. You usually tell them (on the phone) that you have too many clients right now, but since they're here in the limo and drinking martinis, you tell them, "Send me what you have, here's my card, send me your novel or story collection, let's see what you got." The bookstore clerk says she has an historical novel she's been working on since she was Molli's age; the fellow in the jacket says he's written "the new novel."

"And what's that?" Johnny Ray says. "What's that shit?"

"My novel would blow you away, man."

"It would have to be a mighty wind," Molli says, "to blow such a big guy like Johnny Ray away."

Something happens—tires screech, brakes groan, there's a thump and a smash and everyone spills their drinks on themselves. Molli yelps. The limousine has come to a stop.

Seems another limousine—a longer one—has hit the one you're in. The longer limo is filled with drunken prep school boys in blue jackets and red ties. They all have blond hair.

Other cars honk. Cabs, mostly.

The two limo drivers yell at each other, standing in the street.

"What the fuck?" the prep school boys say. "Someone's gonna pay for screwing up our night."

Molli opens the sun roof and pops her head out. "What's with you jack-asses? Can't you hire a driver who can *drive*?"

"Hey, look at the little girl."

Molli sticks out her tongue. She opens her white blouse and flashes her tits at the boys. She giggles and ducks back in the limo.

The boys—half a dozen of them—surround the limo, pound on the windows; they say they want Molli to come out.

"Step out, honey," they say, "we wanna rape you!"

"Hold this," Johnny Ray says, handing you his flask. He walks out of the limo like Godzilla emerging from the ocean. The boys all go quiet. One of them is like, "Oh shit, we're in trouble."

As your star author defends the honor of your other star author by beating the living crap out of the drunk prep school boys, you sniff the flask. Smells like gasoline. You try it; the moonshine burns your mouth and throat but it gives you an immediate buzz, the best you've ever had. So you drink more.

6.

You wake up on a bed in the SoHo Grand. It's six A.M. Molli is next to you, and she's getting up. She's wearing pink pajamas. Johnny Ray is asleep on the floor. Your head is pounding and your eyes hurt. It's your first hangover. "Oh God," you say.

"Don't worry, nothing happened," Molli says. "I have to get a shower. Morning talk show, remember? Go back to sleep."

You close your eyes.

You open your eyes three hours later. Johnny Ray is talking on your cell phone. You sit up.

"He's awake," Johnny Ray says. He holds out the phone. "It's for you. Good news."

"Who is it?"

"L.A."

It's Bernard Goldman. "Hey, guy," he says. "Okay, so Thorn ain't so bad. It's all in the presentation, but the man has talent. Let's seal the deal."

You do some talking, say, "FedEx the paperwork to my office," and you go to the bathroom and piss. You almost puke. Things are still spinning. You don't like this feeling.

Johnny Ray is sitting on the bed and looking out the window. "They're really gonna make a movie of my life," he says. "Weird."

"Where's Molli?"

"She took off to her TV thing. I wanna do TV things."

"What happened last night?"

"Let's see. We got in a fender-bender, I whooped some Central Park rich ass that needed a whooping, we escaped the cops, and you got drunk as a skunk, my friend."

"You didn't do anything with Molli, did you?"

"Oh, man, that's a dumb thing to ask."

"Did I?"

"We had to carry you up here."

"I've never been drunk," you say.

"Welcome to the real world."

"Drunk people do dumb things."

"Look, about Molli," he says. "She's a child. This whole wayward slut thing is an act. A ruse. We talked; she's a virgin. She knows the game. It sells books, right?"

"Right."

"And that's all that matters, right?"

"Right."

"So why don't you get washed up and let's go get us some pancakes?" he says. "Do you like pancakes?" he asks.

"Jonathan," you say, "right now I could eat a whole stack of them. Lots of butter, lots of syrup."

"Breakfast is a very, *very* important thing in a man's life."

You couldn't agree more.

ABOUT THE AUTHOR

MICHAEL HEMMINGSON writes books in every possible genre he can: literary, western, SF, horror, noir, autobiography, erotica, narrative journalism, gonzo journalism, cultural anthropology, critical theory, critifiction, ethnography, and poetry. And private eye yarns. And film and TV studies. He also writes plays and screenplays. He wrote the independent feature film, *The Watermelon*, which you can get on Netflix or Amazon.

ABOUT THE AUTHOR

GARY LOVISI is a Mystery Writers of America Edgar Award nominee and Western Writers of America Spur Award winner. His latest books include *Bad Girls Need Love Too* (Krause), a lovely hardcover showcasing the art of the wildest sexy paperback covers and their outrageous blurbs; *Ultra-Boiled* (Ramble House), which contains twenty-three of his hardest crime stories; *Driving Hell's Highway* (Borgo Press), a hard surreal noir about a lone man driving the back roads of darkest America; *More Secret Adventures of Sherlock Holmes* (Ramble House), collecting three new longer Holmes pastiches; *Gargoyle Nights* (Borgo Press), in which a horrid monster roams the halls of Oldearth's dead; and *Murder of a Bookman* (Borgo Press), where Detective Bentley Hollow investigates murder in the rare book collecting world. Lovisi is the founder of Gryphon Books, editor of *Paperback Parade* and *Hardboiled* magazines, and is the sponsor of an annual paperback book collectors show in New York City, now in its 24th year. To find out more about him his work, or Gryphon Books, visit his web site at: www.gryphonbooks.com.

Borgo Press Books by GARY LOVISI

Driving Hell's Highway: A Crime Novel
Gargoyle Nights: A Collection of Horror
Mars Needs Books!: A Science Fiction Novel
*Murder of a Bookman: A Bentley Hollow Collectibles Mystery
    Novel*
Violence Is the Only Solution: 3 Vic Powers Crime Tales

VIOLENCE IS
THE ONLY SOLUTION

These three Vic Powers stories present hard-boiled dysfunctionality at its most intense and brutal best. These are not tales for the easily squeamish, or those who want to spend their hours leisuring in country-club-style mystery puzzlers. These are the darkest of excursions into taut, tough, nasty crime and noir excesses, featuring a flawed and violent hero whose life leads him on a one-way ride down into the very depths of his own demonic hell!

These are the back alleys of the human heart—filled with shadowy recesses, dirty little secrets, and the occasional gallant gesture of a very human man who's just trying to keep his head above the muck that always is threatening to engulf him. Great crime reading in the 1950s style, where...VIOLENCE IS THE ONLY SOLUTION!

www.ingramcontent.com/pod-product-compliance
Lightning Source LLC
Chambersburg PA
CBHW031401250626
47155CB00004B/1365